TWO DEGREES
HOTTER

de de Cox

Acts 20:35

de de Cox

TWO DEGREES HOTTER

Quantity sales special discounts are available on quantity purchases by corporations, associations, and others. For details, contact the publisher at the address above.

Orders by U.S. trade bookstores and wholesalers. Email info@ BeyondPublishing.net

The Beyond Publishing Speakers Bureau can bring authors to your live event. For more information or to book an event contact the Beyond Publishing Speakers Bureau speak@BeyondPublishing.net

The Author can be reached directly BeyondPublishing.net/AuthordedeCox

Manufactured and printed in the United States of America distributed globally by BeyondPublishing.net

BEYOND
PUBLISHING

New York | Los Angeles | London | Sydney

ISBN: 978-1-949873-96-2

DEDICATION

When most of us think of a dedication, it's typically a thank you of family and friends, but this is different. I want to say thank you to the Sports Card and Gaming Shop in my town. These guys gave the idea of the name of this third book to my son and from there, the rest is history. So thank you to the most amazing card and gaming shop!!!

Photographer:
John Herzog / John Herzog Photography

HMUA:
Joshua Ketron

Swimsuit Wardrobe:
Lisa Opie / Vizcaya Swimwear

Production:
Austin Ozier / Ozier Management

Female Cover Model:
Madison Walker

Male Cover Model:
Bo Cox

Location:
Yorktown Beach, VA

TWO DEGREES
HOTTER

"Willow, stop. Look at me. Did you not think I would find out? Did you not think the truth would reveal itself? Did you not think that this would happen?" Willow could not breathe. Deep in her heart, she knew she could not stop what was about to happen.

Willow looked at Silver and said, "It will not happen because I will not allow it."

Silver laughed heartily. "It will happen, and you will ask for more."

"Never," Willow said.

"Never is a long time, Willow." Silver smiled.

PROLOGUE

Dr. Silver Bleu had told his colleague and good friend, Dr. Nicholas Chrystmas, he would be needing to leave early the evening of the hospital's Mingle and Jingle Gala. He needed to catch a flight early in the morning, so he could arrive in Florida while it was still light to allow Silver time to relax and unpack. Silver quickly made his way through the gala and assured Nick he had packed and was ready for the big conference. And yes, Silver would bring Nick back a souvenir. Silver made sure to thank all of the nurses and staff for a job well done during the year as he walked through the throngs of people.

He looked back one last time. Silver loved the holidays, but he loved the beach, the countryside, and horseback riding even more. The ability to stay in the country while also enjoying the city's extra amenities were all Silver needed.

CHAPTER 1

Silver heard the alarm. It was already time. He grabbed his luggage and got into his car and began the long drive to the airport. His thoughts were of the year and all that he had accomplished, and yet there were still so many goals left unmet. Working at the number one children's hospital in the United States had always been a dream of his. He and Nick had known exactly what the journey they would need to succeed in medical school. They both had made a commitment to be the best pediatric doctors specializing in oncology. It had been hard work and a lot of sacrifice. Silver had sacrificed a lot of time, but the thing he had sacrificed the most were his personal relationships and any intimacy. It was a small pitfall of being a pediatrician, but there were so many more rewards in his career.

Silver considered himself a lady's man. He had an athletic build. His smile made women blush. And he was rather a catch, as some of the nurses at the hospital teased him. One of his best features was that he was a good cook, a really good cook. Silver had won several of the bake-off contests at the hospital, from which he had taken a lot of ribbing from the staff, but he was actually quite proud of the accomplishment. Silver was also not afraid to try new things. He considered himself quite the adventurer. He loved being outdoors and camping, horseback riding, and hiking. Being outdoors was Silver's way of taking a personal time-out. He loved just to sit and watch how the sky changed from dusk to night and the way the stars danced across the heavens.

Silver's old college roommate, Landon Dawson, had offered Silver his home to stay in while Silver was in town for his conference. Landon would come to see him at some point during his stay, and Silver was looking forward to catching up with Landon. Silver pulled into the driveway exhausted. It had been a long flight. He was looking forward to a shower, so he could relax and prepare for the week. It was a warm, Sunday mid-morning.

He noticed another vehicle was already parked next to the house, and Silver wondered if Landon had beat him there. The back driver's side door was open, and a small figure was struggling with something in the backseat. He knew just from the silhouette of the body that this was not Landon. This body belonged to a woman. As he approached the unknown vehicle, he could hear several expletives coming from the woman. Silver had to laugh at the words he overheard. Silver could see she was struggling to get her luggage from the backseat. He stood for just a minute admiring her small stature. He chuckled to himself, just as the young woman backed out with the luggage in full tow.

She immediately looked at Silver and asked, "Are you just going to stand there and stare, or are you going to help?"

Silver recognized that voice. But this beautiful young woman could not be the sassy-pants little sister of Landon. There was just no way. He had not heard or seen little Willow Rainey Dawson for over fifteen years. This definitely was not the little Willow he knew or remembered. Oh, no—this was a very beautiful woman who just happened to be the little sister of his best friend. What had Willow done with her life? And more importantly, what was she doing here now, at the same time he was? This week was going to be interesting indeed.

CHAPTER 2

Silver was enjoying the view that had been placed surprisingly in front of him. He silently laughed to himself when the young female driver, or as he now realized was Willow, asked if he was going to help or not. As he approached her, he knew that she did not recognize him. This conversation could prove eye opening, Silver thought to himself. He decided to feel it out.

"Well, if you would move just to the side a bit, I would be able to help, but there's just one obstacle in the way," Silver said.

Willow looked at him with astonishment and said, "And that is?"

Silver replied, "You. Sweetheart, if you want me to assist in unloading that enormous luggage, which, from the looks of it, is rather heavy, then you need to step to the side, so I can step in." Willow did not hear a single word he said other than that word "sweetheart". No one had ever called her that, except for *one* person in her entire lifetime. The individual had been a close friend of her brother's, but she had not seen him for quite some time.

Willow had just begun her freshmen year of high school when Silver Bleu had made an appearance at their house for the first time. Her brother, Landon, had told their parents that his friend needed a place to go for the holidays because he was unable to travel back home because of the distance and expense. Of course, Landon and Willow's parents were overjoyed with the fact there would be another place setting at the Thanksgiving table. When Silver Bleu had arrived that Tuesday night with Landon, Willow had been immediately love-struck, moon-struck, and any other kind of struck for Landon's new friend.

Willow knew that Silver did not view her as anything other than Landon's little sister. Throughout their years of medical school, Silver would come back with Landon to special events. Willow had watched their friendship grow throughout college and medical school. Silver treated Willow as if she were his own little sister. To get under Willow's skin, Silver would always start his sentences by addressing Willow by "sweetheart". It would irritate Willow most of the time, but as the years passed and Willow grew into her beauty, it became an endearment Willow cherished.

After high school, Willow had decided to pursue interior design. She loved matching and mixing colors from all spectrums with each room. She loved decorating. Interior design was like abstract painting. Willow had left their Wyoming home and broadened her horizons to The New York Interior Design Institute. When Landon had purchased his home in Florida, he had asked Willow to use her magic and make each room unique with a country-based theme. Willow had enjoyed the challenge that had been thrown at her. When completed, not only was she elated about the outcome of her hard work, but so was Landon. He had told Willow that any time she needed to escape the big city and needed to smell the country air; she was more than welcome to stay. Well, Willow had taken her big brother up on his kind offer. She had chosen this week, specifically, because it was during the holidays. Willow would be able to finish the rest of the holiday season with Landon and tell him her exciting news. But as she looked at Silver unloading her luggage, something told Willow these plans were about to be thrown out the window.

As Silver waited for Willow to move, he knew he could get her easily riled up. "Sweetheart, the only way I can help you is if you move, or I move you. Which do you prefer?" His comment brought Willow's thoughts back to the task at hand – she had to move. She did not want Silver to touch her or come anywhere near her. It felt as though the temperature had risen at least two degrees more since Willow had first begun the attempt to remove the luggage.

Before Silver could even grab the handle of the luggage, Willow moved to the front of the car and allowed Silver easy access to her suitcase. Silver pulled it out gently, placed it on its rolling wheels and locked eyes with Willow. "Is there anything else I can help you with, Willow?"

And there he was, staring her right in the face, standing directly in front of her—her first crush, Dr. Silver Bleu. Without thinking, Willow blurted out, "Thank you, but no, Silver. I have it from here."

So, she did recognize him. The fact that Willow recognized him brought a smile to his face.

"And wipe that smile off your face," Willow stated, "and don't call me sweetheart. And by the way, why are you standing in my brother's driveway?"

Silver laughed. So many questions. "I have not seen you for fifteen years, and these are the questions you want to ask me. Well, let's see... The smile is because I am genuinely happy to see you. Calling you sweetheart never fails to get your attention. It always has. And the reason I am standing in your brother's driveway is because I am staying here for at least three weeks while teaching and training the pediatric oncology doctors at the Star Bright Hospital here in Shadow Creek."

Willow could not utter one word. He was here. He was staying. He was happy to see her. He was staying for three weeks. Had she gotten the dates confused with her brother about the availability of his home? Willow looked at Silver and told him not to move. And then reiterated it again. Stay put.

CHAPTER 3

"Stay in plain sight where I can see you. I am going to make a call to Landon to find out what is going on," she said. Silver grinned and nodded his confirmation. Silver knew that no matter what Landon told her, he would not be moving from this driveway. He would be staying the entire three weeks. It was too late to book a hotel near the hospital. Now, if Willow wanted to stay somewhere else, well, then that would be up to her. But Dr. Silver Bleu would not be leaving the premises.

Silver could overhear Willow talking to Landon. He could surmise that Landon may have mixed up a few dates with his little sister. From the *aaaaggggghhh*-ing and the sighing and the placing of her hands on her forehead, Silver knew that that was exactly what had taken place. He heard Willow state "Fine, let me ask him."

Willow looked at Silver and said, "I can only assume that there is no chance of you relocating to a hotel for your time here?"

Silver began to laugh. "You're not serious. All the hotels are booked because of the holidays. No, sweetheart, there is no chance of me relocating a hotel to stay for three weeks. This will do me just fine. Now, you on the other hand, may want to reconsider, just a thought." Willow heard everything up until that word "sweetheart". She really had to talk to Silver about *that one* word.

Willow turned her attention back to Landon on the phone. "Fine, he can stay at one end of your home, and I'll stay at the other end. I cannot believe you mixed the dates," Willow argued with her big brother.

That's all it took for Silver to begin to unpack his rental. He was staying. He needed to unpack. He needed to rest from the flight. As he rolled his luggage past Willow, he heard her inform her big brother, "Landon Dawson, you owe me. You owe me big time."

As Silver began to roll his luggage to the house, he turned to peek back at Willow. She was still unloading some smaller suitcases from the trunk of the car and the passenger seat. What in the world did this woman do for a living? Whatever it was, it required a lot of luggage. Silver shook his head in disbelief. He would be sharing the next few weeks with his best friend's sassy little sister. Well, Silver grinned sheepishly, let the adventures begin. He unlocked the front door and walked through. Into what, he did not know, but he could not wait to find out.

Willow watched the back of Silver as he took off without her. He was not going to help her with the rest of the luggage? Are you kidding me, Willow thought to herself. Where was the chivalry? Where was the helping hand? Where was Silver? He had disappeared inside the house. Just great. She was going to have to lug all of her equipment and suitcases up the driveway without any assistance. Fine. Whatever. She had been doing this by herself since she had taken on this career choice. It may take a few trips, but all would be completed without *his* help.

As Willow placed everything on the front porch, the door opened, and Silver stood in front of Willow with the biggest grin on his face. "Can I help you bring in your luggage?"

"Now, you ask me? After you have watched me unload and carry everything to the porch? Oh, aren't you just the gentleman, Silver? No. I'm good. I can do this all by myself. I do not need your help, or anyone else's for that matter. I just need you to hold the door and stand out of my way." Silver laughed a throaty laugh. He knew he had pushed Willow's button.

And just to add a little cherry on top, Silver replied, "Absolutely, sweetheart."

CHAPTER 4

Oh, this man was incorrigible. Willow could not believe he was standing there holding the door for her. She could not believe Silver was in her brother's home. She had been at a loss for her words when Landon had informed her he had made a mistake, but she could handle it. Willow needed to just get everything inside with no additional comments from *him*. How in the world could Landon make this big of a mistake? Everything had been going smoothly until this. Willow just needed time to herself, but that was not going to happen. He was here and already inside, making himself at home.

As Willow carried, threw, and slung all her luggage into her room, she wondered which of the bedrooms Silver had invaded and marked his own. Willow sat down on the edge of the bed. She remembered what it was like being Landon Dawson's little sister. Most of Landon's friends had been cordial to her, but Silver had seemed to rub her the wrong way when she was younger. Now, at this moment, she was not sure of anything other than the words he had just said "hello sweetheart". She never knew if Silver meant it to be sarcastic or as an endearment. For the most part, she knew Silver was teasing her. Willow had never told anyone (not even her brother, Landon) that she had had a crush on Silver. She knew that Silver had never looked at Willow that way. While Landon was at college, Willow would carry on with life. High school, dances, proms, football and basketball games.

Willow had to admit to herself her favorite part of Landon coming home from college for visits, was not Landon, but *him*. Typically, it was a weekend stay and then Landon and Silver were gone most of the time. They would either attend a sporting event or a concert of some kind. Willow knew that Silver loved country music. Landon, on the other hand, did not. Even though Landon's home was country theme – country music held a bit of sadness. Willow knew why but her brother did not like to discuss. Landon had remained private about his pain. Willow remembered when she first saw Silver. He had had long, flowing, blondish-brown hair. His hair actually looked better than some of Willow's girlfriends. Willow had expected Silver's taste to be more hard-rock and not country. Willow was not surprised often by people's characters or personalities, but Silver had been an enigma. One that she quite could never put her finger on. As the years progressed, and Silver and Landon graduated medical school, Silver and Landon's appearances at her parents' home became less.

After Willow graduated design school in New York, she pursued her Master's in Design. She interned at the Hearth Interior Design Company in Montana, Wyoming, which basically was a company that designed the interiors of log cabins. Imagine that? She truly enjoyed taking the empty and making it full. Though, this trip was to be a vacation. She did not want to think about color scheme. She did not want to peruse through the furniture or color books for the upcoming year. Willow just wanted to enjoy the quietness of Landon's home. But this was not going to happen, and Willow knew it.

CHAPTER 5

Silver chuckled to himself as he heard Willow talking to herself as she unpacked. So far, this trip had not gone as he had planned, but maybe it could be more than he hoped. The bedroom he had chosen while Willow had been attempting to get all her luggage inside was right up to par. It was decorated with a modern country theme. The colors were not too drab or too bright. In Silver's opinion, the forest greens and midnight blues along with the subtle burgundy worked well together. Every accent in the room had been chosen with masculinity in mind, like the paintings of farm life, tractors, and trucks. The best pieces of décor in the room were the actual mule hanes that had been centered over the bed with a picture of two mules in between them. This was heaven. Silver knew he was in his environment. He decided to unpack and see what Willow was up to.

Willow could hear Silver humming. Or was he singing. Either way, it wasn't half bad. Silver had a rough, raspy voice. To a lot of other women, Willow thought, it may even sound husky and sexy or both. To Willow, it was just a bit unnerving. The more she could hear Silver making that noise, the more she became irritated. Why was his singing affecting her this way? Did she have ear buds anywhere? Maybe those would help her drown him out. She looked through her toiletry bag. There was nothing. Absolutely no earbuds were to be found.

As Willow finished placing the last bit of clothing in the closet and putting everything where it belonged in her bathroom, she heard a quiet knock at the door.

Silver's voice came, "You still alive in there?" Willow smiled. At least he had given her time to gather her wits about her after being caught off guard with his presence.

Willow walked to the door and opened it. "Yes, I am alive. I think all has been unpacked and stashed away. If not, I'm sure I'll find it laying somewhere in the bed or on the floor."

Silver grinned. "Well then, let's go to the beach and check things out. Put your swimsuit on. I'll put my trunks on, and we will head out." Willow did not know how to tell him, but she was very hungry. She did not want to go to the beach. She did *not* want to explore the beach with *him*. She wanted to eat first. Willow looked directly into Silver's eyes and said "No. I'm hungry, so the beach can wait. I wonder if Landon has anything or if I need to go out and get a few groceries, or stop and grab a quick sandwich at a local diner?" Silver was taken a bit off guard. No woman had ever told him no. And just like that, Willow had dismissed him and his wants.

"Okay, wait a minute," Silver told Willow. Let's go together to get groceries and then grab a quick bite on the way back home. That way we eliminate any duplication of food. Sound reasonable to you, Willow?" All Willow heard was him offering to go together. Silver watched as Willow thought about the question. He wondered what she was thinking.

After a few seconds passed, Willow said "Why not? Let's get this over with."

CHAPTER 6

Silver laughed, "Sweetheart, it's not going to be all that bad. I'll be with you. You'll see that grocery shopping will be taken to new heights with me. Don't worry, it will be pain free." Silver knew that he always had Willow's attention when he used his pet name for her.

Willow smiled. "It's not that. It's just such a routine with groceries."

"What do you mean," Silver asked.

"Well," Willow began, "You have to go to the grocery store. You have to take the items off the shelves. You have to place the items in your cart. You have to check out, where the items are rung up and returned to you, just to be put back in the cart. Then, you have to push the cart to the car where you then take the items out of the cart and put them in the car, just so you can travel home and take the items out of the car and into the house and put them away into the cabinets. It's such a chore. It just seems ridiculous to me sometimes, and then it's a repeat every week."

Silver started laughing and could not stop. "I've never heard grocery shopping explained in such graphic detail, but we could just order online and go pick it up. That would knock out several steps. Would that make your life easier, Willow?" Willow knew Silver was teasing her, but she nodded her head and said yes anyway.

Silver leaned in, and without even thinking about what he was doing or the consequences, he kissed Willow. A quick kiss was all it was. No longer than a second.

Willow stepped back and looked Silver dead in the eyes. "What was that?"

Silver laughed, "I hope it was a kiss. Have you never been kissed before?" Willow did not want to answer that. She had been kissed, of course. She just could not remember when it had happened last.

"Well, it accomplished what I hoped it would," Silver chuckled.

"And that was what?"

"You are no longer worried about grocery shopping. Your thoughts have now been turned to when I will kiss you next."

Willow scoffed. "I doubt that, Silver, but you can think what you want." Silver watched as Willow began to blush slightly.

"It's ok, Willow. Trust me, there will be a next time."

"Never again," Willow replied sternly.

"Well, we are getting nowhere fast," Silver told Willow. He turned and walked back into the living room. "Let's get this job taken care of because I am famished, and I know you are as well."

Willow followed him. "And just how do you know I'm famished?"

"Trust me, I just know."

"I hate to admit it, but yes, I am a bit hungry." Silver laughed and pulled out his computer to order everything they would need for their stay. The groceries would be ready within two hours, which gave them enough time to eat beforehand.

As they headed outside, Willow turned to lock the door just as Silver turned to do the same. Their hands touched for just a moment. That small touch sent shivers down Willow's spine. Silver noticed and asked if Willow was cold, but he knew his touch had affected Willow. Shoot, her touch had done a whammy on Silver, too.

Willow pulled her hand back quickly. "If you have the keys, go ahead and lock up."

"As you wish, Willow," Silver grinned.

Silver walked towards his car while informing Willow they would take his car since she was parked in front of him. He walked to the passenger side and clicked the fob to open it.

"Well, well," Willow said. "Chivalry is not dead."

"Of course not, Willow. I'm here to impress. Did it work?" Willow just couldn't help herself – she burst out laughing.

"I give, Silver. I give. You win. Let's just get something to eat and pick up the groceries."

CHAPTER 7

Silver got in and started the car. "Don't forget your seatbelt, ma'am." Willow grinned and clicked her seatbelt into place just as they began to pull out of the driveway. Silver looked over at her as she rummaged through her purse. He watched Willow take everything out and lay the items her lap. There were some very unusual items in Willow's purse. He saw a measuring tape, a small level, an industrial stapler. There was nothing girly inside her purse. There was nothing personal that he could see, either. The curiosity was killing him.

Silver could not resist the question he was about to ask Willow. It would set the mood for lunch, so Silver had to tread carefully. "Willow, I just want to ask a question. I've been watching you organize your purse for the past ten minutes. I was expecting lipstick, lip gloss, hand lotion, a brush, or even a tweezers, but needless to say, you have me totally perplexed."

"Yeah, I need those items," Willow told Silver. "The items you named off are just icing on the cake. But, I am not a cake, so I don't need any icing. My career requires that I'm prepared at all times whenever I walk into a home." Silver was listening intently, which Willow found, if she admitted to herself, quite refreshing. Most of the time, as soon as she started to talk shop, interest waned. "I am fortunate in the fact that my job does not require me to wear cosmetics to make a sale. My job is to look at a room and knowing how to add or take away one or two pieces to make it fit my clients' needs." Silver was just dying to ask, and he knew Willow could see the question forming in his eyes.

"Yes, Silver, I am an interior designer. My area of expertise is country, log cabin themes. I have worked extensively in Montana, Wyoming with Hearth Interior Design for the past five years. They are one of the top ten design companies in the United States, focusing primarily in the log cabin industry. I have been blessed to travel all over the world."

Silver continued to look expectantly at Willow and said "Go on. Tell me more. What happens when you find a client and a home to decorate?"

"I listen to their specific ideas of how they want their home to look. I listen to how they want family or friends to feel when they first walk into their home. I make notes about their favorite colors and favorite designs. From there, I forward the bid and the design for each room, and I take it from there. If you love what you are doing, it's not that difficult to do every day. I love taking something that has nothing inside of it and then placing décor inside to recreate their memories. Your home is your heaven. Your home should be where you find peace and solace from the wicked ole world we live in daily."

Silver could not help but be mesmerized by Willow's voice, but also with the fact that she genuinely cared about her clients' needs. He did not want to admit this to Willow, but he was intrigued by her explanation of her career. He needed Willow's help desperately in the area of interior design for his home. Silver wondered why Landon had never mentioned how successful his little sister had become. He made a mental note to ask Landon the next time he saw him.

Willow looked at Silver. "Anything else, Mr. Bleu? I'm an open book. Just ask a question and I will answer to the best of my ability." Silver laughed. Willow was the little sister of his best friend. Willow had become a beautiful woman who was not only mesmerizing but also very intelligent. Willow had peaked Silver's interest even more. Silver could not wait to eat, get the groceries, and return home, so he would have Willow all to himself in Landon's home. The thought that he wanted to spend time alone with Willow surprised him. His heart was beating a bit fast. Being a doctor, and always trying to practice what he preached, Silver was diligent with his health checkups. He was in fit shape both mentally and physically. But as far as emotionally, there were probably several of Silver's friends who would agree *that* he needed to be rechecked.

He smiled and looked at Willow. "I think we are off to a great start, Willow. Thank you for sharing a bit of your life with me. Let's get something to eat."

CHAPTER 8

As Silver cruised down the streets of the small town of Dove's Landing, Willow researched cafes for them to enjoy lunch on her phone. Out of the corner of her eye, Willow finally took the time to really look at Silver. Silver had piled his hair atop his head in a messy bun. From what Willow could see, Silver's hair was very long. It fit his personality, Willow thought to herself. She could only imagine what kind of pediatric doctor Silver made. Silver had dark blue eyes, almost as if the sea waters had painted them. Willow could not wait to see how long his hair truly was and the full color. It was as if Silver's hair had been kissed by the sun with many hues of blonde. Willow admitted to herself that Silver was quite good looking. Silver could feel Willow's eyes upon him. He felt he would give her to time to see if she liked what she was seeing.

Silver unexpectedly asked Willow if she had found a café for them to have lunch. Willow shook herself back to reality. "Yes, I think I found one that is around the corner here. Just take a right at the next light. It's called the Back Home Café. They have dining inside or outside. Since it's so pretty, I would love to eat outside," Willow suggested. Silver had been thinking the same thing. It was too gorgeous a day to remain inside.

"Sounds like a plan," he replied. They parked on the side of the street, and Silver jumped out and opened Willow's door. She was still trying to place everything back in her purse. Silver laughed and said, "I don't think we will need those things, but if they must come with us, I'll wait for you to put everything back together." Willow blushed with embarrassment.

"I'm sorry. I just never know when I will need one of them."

"It's ok, sweetheart. I understand. They are a part of you. Let's enjoy this day and our meal." Willow was surprised Silver had noticed and made the comment. She had encountered several men who did not appreciate nor understand her career choice or her passion for interior design.

"I agree," Willow replied with an exuberant smile. "I'm starving." As they began to walk towards the Back Home Café, Willow could not help but notice the intricacy of the cobblestone path that led to the doors. The landscaping had been tastefully done so the ambience reflected a country feel. When Silver opened the doors, it was as if Willow had been taken back to her childhood.

The red and white tables were square with rounded corners and silver coil surrounding the entire perimeter of the table. The chairs were encased in the red vinyl covers with the same silver metal trim as the table. As Willow began to review the room and its décor—what she did with every place she visited— she noticed a soda fountain to the right of the entrance. Willow was extremely excited to try it out. She gently reached for Silver's hand to get his attention, but instead, Silver's pinky finger intertwined with her own. Another shiver went through Willow.

"Yes, sweetheart, I already saw it. I could see your enthusiasm as soon as you laid eyes on it. Come on. Let's not waste one minute." Silver guided Willow to the soda foundation by gently tugging her behind him, all the while not untangling their pinky fingers. As Silver looked for a place to sit, he could not help but smile to himself. He had felt Willow shiver. He knew she had felt something when he had touched her. He was going to enjoy lunch.

He found a spot and patted the stool. "How's this?" Silver asked. "Will this do?" Willow nodded. Silver was going to allow Willow to sit first, but she had not let go of his pinky yet. He looked at Willow and said, "Do you want to give my pinky back to me? We can hold to each other as long as you want. You decide, Willow."

Willow looked at their linked pinkies and said, "I'm sorry. She gently let go, but felt empty as soon as she did. As they sat and looked at their menus, Silver watched Willow intently try to decide what she would like.

He leaned into her and said, "I think I'll do the BLT and chips. You can never go wrong with a sandwich that has held the test of time. Also, I'm going to try the coke with a splash of vanilla. What are you going to get?" he asked.

"I'm thinking about the crack burger with the special secret homemade sauce and chips. And if I know this country café, their sweet tea is what Landon would describe as liquid diabetes." Silver burst out laughing.

CHAPTER 9

Landon had always had the best, quirky sayings. Silver knew the relationship Willow had with her brother. There were plenty of times Silver had come home with Landon from college. The first time Silver had met Willow the door had opened, and Willow had just about knocked both him and Landon down. She had been a ball of energy. Willow knew that if she needed to discuss her school day with Landon, he was just a text or call away, but when Landon came in from college, it was Willow's time with him. Their parents knew they wanted the time to catch up.

Willow shook herself back to the present. "I'm ready if you are," Willow informed Silver.

"I'm ready as well," he said. Silver seriously doubted that Willow knew what he was thinking. If she did, she probably would not remain sitting at the table to have lunch with him. Contrary to how Silver had remembered Willow, she was nothing near that awkward teenager. Silver had to keep reminding himself she was Landon's little sister, and Landon was one of his best friends.

Silver remembered a comment from his dad, "Is it really worth the friendship that you may lose?" Those words had not meant much at the time he had heard them, but now Silver knew what his father meant. Sometimes love did not conquer all. He had learned the hard way that some things were just not meant to be. Silver had dated on and off throughout college, but he had not had a lot of time to invest in relationships. After graduating medical school and interning at Pioneer Children's Hospital, his career had taken a front seat. Silver did not have any complaints, though. He had met some of the most amazing individuals at Pioneer Children's Hospital. While Silver had his fair share of dates, there just had not been anything serious enough to write home about. He and Dr. Nicholas Chrystmas were considered the most prominent pediatric oncology doctors in the United States. Silver knew that establishing a relationship with a woman would require someone who understood his time and commitment, not just with reference to his career, but also to the children he treated. His relationship status had not changed, but one never knew, Silver thought to himself as he looked at Willow. Things in life could change at any given second.

"Well, let's order and enjoy this lunch before we head to pick up the groceries," Silver stated. Throughout the lunch, Willow and Silver made small talk about each of their current jobs. Nothing was mentioned about the past and there were no comments made about the future. It was nice just to relax and enjoy the good conversation with no expectations.

As they finished, Silver knew Willow had enjoyed the meal. And from all accounts of the conversation, she had enjoyed catching up. Willow smiled at Silver and asked, "Should we order dessert?"

Silver chuckled and wanted to say, "you're all the dessert that I need", but he knew that would not fly with Willow. Besides, he knew how corny that would be. Silver was not much of a dessert guy. Silver looked at Willow and told her no, he was okay, but if she wanted to order something sugary, she could be his guest. Willow smiled and ordered a piece of strawberry cheesecake with the syrup just dripping off the edges and oozing onto the plate.

CHAPTER 10

Good lord, what was Willow doing to him? She was painting his mind with thoughts of her, strawberries, and syrup. They definitely needed to leave and the quicker, the better, or Silver was going to make a fool of himself. "I made sure I got it all," Silver replied.

Willow took the last bite of cheesecake and licked every bit of what was stuck to the fork very slowly. Silver was never going to make it back to that car in one piece. As Willow placed her fork and napkin onto the table, Silver noticed just a small bit off strawberry syrup had found its way to the corner of Willow's luscious, pouty lips.

Silver could not resist. "Willow come here." And before she could ask why, her body betrayed her and leaned in to find out what Silver needed. It happened so quickly that Willow had to replay the incident over in her head. Silver gently took his thumb and wiped the syrup from her lips. He licked his thumb free of the syrup and looked at her.

"You were right. It was delicious." She began to blush. It was the pinkest of pink. She nervously checked her mouth for any more remaining syrup. "No need to do that. I made sure I got it all."

Willow tried to rise to leave, but her legs would not cooperate. They felt like she had just taken roller skates off. It felt like she was floating on air. What was happening to her? Why was she reacting this way to Silver? Was she coming down with something? Maybe she should ask Silver to see if she had a slight fever? No, that would not be good. That would mean he would have to touch her again. She could barely even stand after the last time. Willow felt like she was teenager again and seeing Silver for the very first time.

Snap out of it, Willow thought to herself. It was just Silver. No big deal. This was Landon's best friend. Even Willow and Landon's parents loved Silver. It was as if Landon and Silver were brothers in real life. Sometimes there would be a bit of drama when they both came home, but overall, it was the typical sibling disagreements. Willow knew that Silver had remained in touch with their parents because they would tell Landon a few tidbits about Silver's career and what was taking place in his life.

Silver stood up and as he did, he gently placed his hand in the middle of Willow's back to turn her around on her stool. Silver was, admittedly, curious to see what this next leg of their journey would hold for the day. The grocery pick-up should be easy since all had been ordered online.

Walking back to the car, he noticed Willow had pulled her cell phone out of her purse and was texting rapidly. Silver asked if everything was okay.

"Yes, it's just Landon texting me about mom's progress and how dad has been a trooper staying on top of all the doctor's visits," Willow commented.

Silver had remembered while visiting with Landon that their mother had undergone chemo treatments for ovarian cancer after she had been diagnosed while Landon was in college and Willow at home. The doctors had treated it aggressively. Based on the last time Landon had spoken to Silver about how his mother was doing, all was well. The chemo had worked, and their mom had been cancer free for two years.

But the look of concern on Willow's face made Silver feel uneasy. He did not know if he should push the question or wait for Willow to answer. Darn the wait, he needed to know. "Willow, is she okay? Do we need to go back to Landon's? Do you need some time to make a call? I can wait in the car, if you need some privacy alone."

"No, Mom is ok. Landon just wants me to check on them when we return to the house. Silver understood the "check on" phrase. He had heard it too many times while at Pioneer Children's Hospital. There was always a "check on".

"Alright. Then, let's go pick up the groceries, head back to the house, unload, and relax for the evening. I know you are tired from the drive. I know I am." Willow did not want to admit it, but she was not just tired, she was completely exhausted. She nodded in agreement.

CHAPTER 11

They drove to the grocery store, and Silver checked into their online order to let the workers know they had arrived. They did not have to wait long before an employee brought their goods out to their car. Silver, attempting to make small talk with the employee, asked how the man's day was going. He answered, "Busier than a cat with puppies." Silver had heard this phrase only one other time. Willow's dad had been remodeling their home and had dropped paint onto the hardwood floor, had put an indent in the hall wall, and purchased the wrong size sheet set. As Landon and Silver had walked through the door, Landon had asked his father what in the world was going on. Landon's father reply was that same "busier than a cat with puppies". Both Landon and Silver had barely been able to stop laughing. Their laughter was so uncontrollable that even Landon's dad had joined in until they each had tears in their eyes. Those were moments that Silver would remember forever.

Silver felt Willow tug at his arm. "Silver, where'd you go? she asked. He shook himself.

"Just thinking back to a memory with your dad." Willow watched as Joseph, the employee, loaded the vehicle. Finally, Joseph finished and handed Willow a clipboard for her to sign they had received their order. After signing, she looked at Silver and asked, "Ready to go?"

"Yes, ma'am."

"Home to Oz, please." Willow smiled. She truly had enjoyed the day with Silver. She had to admit she was a bit leery of Silver's charm, but he had been a true gentleman.

They drove back in silence. And that was okay. Each was caught up in their own thoughts about the day. The drive was quiet and beautiful as they drove along the landscape of the beach. They pulled into their driveway. Silver told Willow if she would unlock the front door, he would bring the groceries in, and they could unload and put them all away together. Willow heartily agreed and within 15 minutes, the task had been accomplished. All the groceries were placed in the cabinets.

Willow tried to think of things to do. She knew she could not call Landon yet because of the time difference. He was not off work yet. She really needed to finish discussing the vacation fiasco with him.

Willow looked around the kitchen and then looked at Silver, who was watching her. His brows were drawn together. I wonder what he is thinking, Willow thought to herself. And then, without warning, Silver asked Willow if she needed to take a quick cat nap. He was tired from flight and was thinking about just resting his eyes for a few moments.

Willow smiled. "Yes, Silver, I think a "cat nap" would be do me good." Silver just quickly replied with a "sweet dreams".

CHAPTER 12

Well, that was way too easy, Willow thought as she walked to her room. The bed looked so inviting, her mind went to the task Landon had given her–call Mom. Willow dialed the number and waited.

She heard her dad answer, "Hello, baby girl, how are you doing?" Willow immediately felt her dad's immense pleasure in hearing her voice.

"I'm well Daddy, and how is Momma?"

Her dad stated matter-of-factly, "She's fine. She's resting, plus she's got me." Willow laughed. Her mom and dad were *that* couple everyone talked about. Her friends would always comment, "I hope I find this kind of love". Willow knew their love was special. After confirming all was well, Willow told her dad to tell mom that she loved her and if they needed anything to give her a call. Just knowing that her mom was resting, Willow could let out the deep breath she had been holding in. Admittedly, she was worn out. She changed into her most comfortable sweats. The bed was inviting her. Right now, any bed would do. Willow curled up on the bed and was out before her head hit the pillow.

Silver did not know how long his cat nap had lasted, but it felt longer than 15 minutes. Silver did feel rested. A shower would be nice. Silver walked into his bathroom and turned the hot water on until he felt the steam rising. The water felt nice rolling down his face and back. He had no idea how long he stayed in the shower, but when he finally stepped out, he felt so good, like he could run a sprint. He grabbed a towel, which perfectly wrapped around his entire body since Landon was about the same size as him. As he walked into the bedroom, he felt a twinge of hunger. Maybe just a quick snack. He thought to himself. Since he and Willow had purchased a few snacks, he decided to do a bit of scavenging as to what was good. He could not hear anything throughout the house, so Silver assumed Willow was still napping. The walk to the kitchen was silent until he turned the corner and heard Willow. The young woman was just not sleeping, though. She sounded like a chain saw cutting logs. He laughed. It was a hearty laugh. For someone so petite and cute, this caught Silver off guard. She must have been zonked. There was no way Silver would dare wake her. There was no wrath like a woman who has been awoken from her nap.

CHAPTER 13

Silver opened the refrigerator door and pulled out the ingredients for a sandwich. Even though they had eaten about four hours ago, Silver was starving. After everything was dressed and on his plate, Silver turned to leave the kitchen, but standing in the doorway of the kitchen, was Willow.

"Well, well, Chef Bleu. What other surprises do you have up your sleeve? Willow teased.

Silver smiled charmingly. "There is nothing up my sleeve, sweetheart, for I'm not wearing sleeves. Only this towel." Willow began to blush. From what Willow could gather, there was nothing beneath the bath towel.

Silver immediately noticed the blush rising to Willow's cheeks and responded, "But I'll leave that to your imagination."

He paused.

Would you like me to fix you something? It won't take me but a minute. With all the groceries we picked up, it's a regular smorgasbord. Your choice. Just let me know." Silver noticed that Willow's eyes had not lowered from his. He could tell she felt a bit uncomfortable.

"Willow, it's ok. I'll go get dressed and return in something more suitable to eat a sandwich with you. Everything is in the fridge. Just grab some chips, and a drink, and then we'll go outside on the deck and enjoy the sounds of the waves."

Willow knew he knew that she had not removed her eyes from his. She was not going to allow herself to look anywhere else. Especially where her eyes did not need to roam. She nodded in agreement with Silver and watched him walk slowly from the kitchen. She was ready to wipe that smirk off his face.

Willow prepared a sandwich for herself along with her favorite cheese puffs. At the moment, she was not concerned with her carb intake, she just wanted something light and cool. As she was opening the doors, Silver appeared in khaki shorts. Just in khaki shorts. No shirt and no shoes. Willow had known Silver was fit and had an athletic build. He had been like that since the first time she had met him. And he had not changed. Silver saw her reviewing his choice of clothing and asked if everything met with her approval or did he need to add a shirt or shoes.

Willow thought to herself, could she eat with Silver? He was half-naked. But for some reason, his appearance did not make her feel uncomfortable. Actually, it made her feel… funny. She could not quite put her finger on why, but she enjoyed looking at Silver's physique.

They ate their snacks while talking about their view. It was a warm evening with a slight breeze, but it was not humid. The waves were lapping on the shore and one could feel the soft whisper of the wind.

Willow closed her eyes. The day was coming to an end. It had been quite an eventful day that was still continually surprising her.

Silver looked at Willow with her eyes closed. "I could spend the night out here. We could wake up to the sun rising and watching the colors dance across the water."

She was caught by the word "we". She looked at Silver incredulously. Where in the world would they sleep? Silver told her to let her creativity as an interior designer take control. Was that not what she did? She took a room and turned it upside down with color, design and character. A deck was just a room without four walls. He knew she could do it. He looked at Willow and winked at her.

"Not up to the challenge, sweetheart?" There it was. That word. He knew how it got under Willow's skin.

Willow saw right through him. She gathered their plates and cups and took them to the kitchen. She came back out, placed her hands on her hips, and stated matter-of-factly, "Oh, I'm up for it. I know you probably still have some matters to prepare for your big conference. So why don't you just go inside and do whatever doctors do, and I'll get the *creative juices* flowing."

Silver could not help but laugh. It was a genuine laugh. He looked at her stance and knew she meant business. "Fine, fine. I do have a few notes that I need to go over and tweak just a bit of info regarding my statistics." He walked into the kitchen and closed the door behind him. He turned to watch her through the window, but she caught him with a look of exasperation.

"I can't do this with you constantly hovering! Go be a doctor, Silver, please," Willow pleaded with him.

43

CHAPTER 14

Before she could say anything else, Silver had disappeared into the den. She heard the television being turned on. She peeked out of the corner of her eye and saw him return to the recliner with a computer in hand and a remote in the other. Good, Willow thought. This would allow her time to begin the preparations to turn the deck into a nighttime camping adventure.

She looked at the furniture and envisioned where she would move the pieces and what she would add to give it the camping atmosphere. Willow remembered there was a tent in the garage the family had used. Willow's dad loved camping and enjoyed the outdoors. His love of camping, the outdoors, and the smell of a crisp evening had been shared with Willow and Landon. She knew what she wanted to trim the deck with. She just needed to find the old coal oil lanterns. Willow found them in the corner where her dad would always hide things from her mom, just as she knew they would be. Placed beside the lanterns were some neatly rolled sleeping bags and to her surprise, so were some Halloween string lights. Willow prayed they would work. She turned one strand on. It lit up. This was going well. Willow brought everything back to the deck and began the transformation. She hoped Silver would like what she had done in such a short amount of time and with limited décor.

Silver could see Willow walking back and forth with items and dropping them on the deck, then leaving and returning again. She was very intent and determined in her walk. He could not wait to see how she was going to transform the deck. He would give her all the time she needed. She was in her element. He could tell. She had been talking and singing the entire time Silver had been inside. He enjoyed listening to her. Silver thought she may be a distraction while he was working, but instead he was more focused on his agenda and itinerary than he wanted to admit.

He watched her as she wiped her hands on the back of her shorts and then turned to walk inside. He did not look up from his computer. Silver heard her light steps on the kitchen floor and heard her stop and clear her voice –

"Ready or not, let's do this," she said.

Silver smiled. "I cannot wait to see what your touch and expertise have done to the deck." With that, Silver stood up. "Lead the way."

Willow told him, "You have to close your eyes. No peeking. I want you to be surprised, Silver. This is what I love, a challenge. Cover your eyes, please, and I'll lead you to the deck." Silver felt like a child at a surprise birthday party. Everyone knew there was a party taking place. You just didn't know when the family would jump out. "

Okay, eyes closed. I'm going to count to three and then you can open. Put your hands over your eyes," Willow pleaded. "Stand right here. I have to step away to do something special so that you can get the full effect."

Silver felt Willow leave his side. He kept his hands over his eyes. Silver heard the patter of her feet running all over the deck.

Willow kept looking back to be sure that Silver was not peeking. She had taken the Halloween lights and strung them around deck like garland during. Willow had then taken the lanterns and placed them in each of the four corners of the deck so that a bit of glimmer encompassed the entire deck. The sleeping bags were laid neatly in the middle. Willow had placed some fruit and red wine on the table, neatly decorated with a garnishment to accentuate the evening.

Willow had to admit she was quite proud of her accomplishment. She hoped that Silver would feel as much elation as she did.

Willow positioned Silver and told him to take a look. Silver could tell Willow was a bit hesitant to have him remove his hands from his eyes. He was a little unsure as well. When he removed his hands and saw the change, he could not believe Willow had done something so exceptional. She had changed the entire deck into a beautiful atmosphere that perfectly captured the sun's evening rays. It was if an artist had taken the canvas and brushed the magnificent colors of the sunset onto the deck.

Willow was watching Silver to see his reaction. She knew she had done exceptionally well. He turned to Willow and, without any hesitancy, said, "I've never seen anything so extraordinary."

CHAPTER 15

All the emotions Willow had been holding in since arriving that morning and all that had happened since came flowing out like the rushing waves of the ocean before her. It started as one little tear and then another until she could not stop crying. She was so worn out. Willow was especially worried about her mom. She just needed to cry, and she could not stop the tears.

Silver saw the first little tear slowly slide down her beautiful cheek. He did not know if Willow was so emotional about the transformation or what had happened since he opened his eyes to see the warm display of colors on the deck.

"Hey," Silver looked at her. "What's wrong? What happened? I swear, Willow, it's unbelievable. I had no idea the talent you kept hidden. Your ability to take a blank canvas and transform it into something so warm and inviting, I honestly had no idea. I'm sorry if I teased you. I'm sorry if I did not take your career seriously," Silver told her.

Willow gently smiled and tried to wipe the tears away. It was not working. Silver walked towards her and said, "Come here sweetheart." Willow could not move. Her emotions had completely taken over and she was just spent. Without hesitation, Silver pulled Willow into his arms. Those arms were masculine and virile. Silver felt her heartbeat against his chest. "It's ok, Willow. I'm here. It's going to be ok," Silver kept repeating. When Silver looked down into Willow's beautiful eyes, he became lost. He was pulled into the look of worry and weariness that filled her face. It was the look of the lost little girl he remembered from so long ago. Silver kissed her forehead, then kissed her tears away, then gently, like the toss of a feather on the wind, kissed her succulent lips. She did not pull away, but she did not open herself to him. He knew better. This was not the moment to continue the kiss, or anything else.

Silver knew Willow just needed a calming moment, so he just pulled her tighter into his arms and did not let go. He felt her give in and relax against him. Willow did not want to move from the warmth and the security of Silver's arms or embrace. It just felt right. She did not want to question why. She just needed to feel that all was going to be okay, and Silver made her feel this way.

Silver did not know how long they stood in that one spot on the deck, but he knew Willow had calmed down. Silver could tell by the sound of Willow's breathing she was relaxed against him.

He placed his chin on top of Willow's head as reassurance he was there. Willow breathed in his scent. He was there. He was with her.

Willow stepped back and looked at Silver. "Thank you. I don't know what came over me."

Silver looked deeply into her eyes. "I'm not going anywhere, Willow. I'll remain as long as you need me.

Let's sit for a minute on the steps. We can enjoy the rest of the evening and your workmanship."

He led her down to the deck steps and sat on them.

"Listen to the waves," Willow said. "They are music to my ears. As the tide comes in, you can inhale the delightful scent of the wind wafting through the breeze, and you can hear the lap of the waves on the sand. It's mesmerizing."

Silver had to agree. The evening was very soothing. One that he had not experienced in a long time.

The sun began to slowly set. Willow commented on how it would touch the tip of the earth before it slowly disappearing into the midnight blue sky.

The evening faded and all that was left was to rise and go back inside.

CHAPTER 16

Willow leaned against Silver's strong shoulder and whispered a small thank you.

Without moving, Silver said, "Any time. I will always be here for you."

As Willow rose, she told Silver she was tired. She would be going to bed and would see him in the morning before he left for the conference. She asked Silver politely if he wanted her to fix breakfast, but he shook his head.

"I typically do not eat breakfast. I'll try not to disturb you. I'll be gone most of the day, but I should be home around six in the evening. We can cook something together then," he offered.

Willow loved to cook, but she rarely had the inclination to just cook for one. She agreed with Silver and each walked into their own bedroom. It was already difficult to keep her eyes open as she changed and brushed her teeth.

Silver watched as Willow closed the door. He did not know how the morning was going to go or the next three weeks of the medical conference, but he did not think he would be able to remain distant from Willow. When Silver held Willow, there had been a moment that Silver felt something unknown to him. Silver had been unable to give thought to anything other than Willow. Overwhelmed with these thoughts, Silver prepared for the morning and was asleep as soon as he laid down..

Willow's alarm went off. The snooze button. Where was the snooze button? Just another ten minutes, Willow thought. After 20 minutes, Willow knew she needed to get up. This was to be her vacation. Her vacation by herself. Her vacation where there was no one else in Landon's home. But this was not the case. *He* was here. He was here in Landon's house with her. He had interrupted her vacation. How in the world had Silver Bleu turned her world upside down?

Willow could see it was a vibrant, glorious morning and decided there was no better way to start the day than with a run on the beach. in her running gear As she was turning towards the sink to fill it, she noticed a small note to the side of the counter. Willow picked it up and written were the words "Enjoy the sun and the day. I'll be home later to help with dinner. Silver".

For the first time in a long time, Willow felt secure. She did not know if it was due to the words or the man. Either way, the morning could not have started out any better.

Willow walked down to the beach just as the sun began to rise. She stopped. The sand was cool on her bare feet. There was a light breeze keeping the morning crisp. A shiver went through Willow's entire being. She sat down, and in the quiet of the early morning, she watched and listened as God's omnipotent presence washed over her.

Willow and Landon had been raised in the church by their parents. She remembered all the traditions they had grown up with because of this— fall festivals, turkey dinners, bingo nights with family and friends. She had veered from attending church when she left for college but had held to her faith in God's existence. During the dark times when their mother had been going through chemotherapy, there had been many a night when Willow would sit in the hospital chapel. She did not know how to pray for the miracle needed, but she knew prayer was what was needed most.

This sunrise reminded her of that unknowing faith of God's constant presence. Landon did not speak much about his faith to his family. Willow knew he, too, had prayed in the hospital chapel, but Landon was very private. Growing up, Willow had always known where to find Landon when something went awry. The barn and the horses called his name. Landon loved the country life.

The waves moving forward caught Willow's attention. She jumped up and began her warmups for her run.

Silver had left in the wee hours. He had tried his best not to make too much noise while gathering everything he needed for the first day of the conference. He packed a lunch because he knew he would not have time to leave Star Bright Hospital all day. He decided to leave a note for a Willow. He was not sure why he left the note. He just felt he should leave a message.

CHAPTER 17

As Silver was pulling into the hospital parking lot, he wondered what Willow would do during the day. He caught himself. Why are you thinking of Willow? He asked himself. He would be speaking to over 100 pediatric oncologists from around the country and he needed to be prepared. He parked and grabbed his briefcase which held his laptop and other conference materials.

Silver walked through the hospital doors. Children's hospitals were always bright and cheery. As Silver walked towards the information desk, he could tell the walls had been painted by children. More than likely had been painted by the child patients at Star Bright Hospital.

He knew he was headed in the right direction when he saw a rather large group heading down the hallway into a room marked "auditorium". Silver took off down the hallway, following the masses. It was going to be a rather large crowd it appeared. Silver laughed to himself. He sure hoped he could keep all entertained and informed of the new technology. He did not want to appear boring.

After entering the auditorium, he perused the attendees. He saw many incredible doctors all who had dedicated their careers to changing and finding a cure for pediatric cancers. Before he could walk the steps to the stage, he felt a hand on his shoulder and heard a familiar voice say, "What's going on, Dr. Bleu?" Silver knew that voice, but there was no way it could be his college roommate. It could not be Dr. Landon River Dawson.

Landon clapped Silver on his back. "Man, it is good to see you!"

"It's good to see you, too, Landon," Silver replied. "What are you doing here? I thought you could not make it. Last time we talked, you did not know if you could get away to attend!"

Landon chuckled. "I heard there was going to be this "famous" pediatric oncologist, and everyone was raving about him. I had to see if he was real." Silver could not help but laugh wholeheartedly.

"I sure hope he's as good as they say," Silver replied.

"I sure hope so. I didn't drive all this way to waste my time.

Afterwards, let's get caught up. I cannot wait to hear how my little sister is treating you." Silver immediately agreed.

The first day of the conference ran smoothly. Silver answered all the questions that were asked of him. Many connections were made. And for today, everyone seemed very enthusiastic for the next day's topic of discussion.

As Silver was leaving, Landon caught up with him. "Let's head back to the house. We'll talk to Willow and see what she wants for dinner and take it from there!"

As Silver pulled into the driveway, he could see that Willow's car was still in the same spot she had left it when she first arrived. H could not help but wonder what she had been up to.

Landon parked behind him. Before either of them could get halfway up the drive, Willow came bounding out from the side of the house, scaring them both half to death. She was in jean shorts— *very* short shorts— and a lemon bikini top. She jumped into Landon's arms and hugged him tight. "I've missed you, big brother! I didn't expect you to come right away and take care of the problem," she said, looking at Silver.

"Me? I'm not the problem, sweetheart," Silver smiled. "It must be you." Willow could tell that Silver was joking and teasing her. Landon watched the display of banter and knew that something was up. What, he did not know, but something was definitely happening between his best friend and little sister.

Landon placed Willow back on the ground. "Well, from what I see, you're not in eminent danger. Are you?"

"Not yet," Silver remarked with a sly wink at Willow.

Willow could tell the conversation was going nowhere, and she wanted to talk to Landon privately about this situation he had placed her in.

"Come on guys. I'm famished. Let's go inside and see what we can scrounge up for dinner." Both Landon and Silver looked at each other. She had not changed.

CHAPTER 18

As Willow entered the kitchen, she had no idea if she could "scrounge" something up or if they needed to order delivery. She did not want to cook inside. Willow wanted to grill outside. As Silver and Landon looked at her, she smiled and suggested just that. Silver had been thinking the same thing. He loved eating outside. Landon nodded his head in agreement.

Willow ordered Silver to take out the steaks they had purchased. She would cut some vegetables and they could skewer them and then roast them. "Whatever you say, sweetheart," Silver replied. Willow expected herself to be angry at the name, but this time was different. There was a different meaning behind it.

The meal was delicious. It was nice just to sit, relax, and shoot the breeze, as Willow's dad would say. The day was ending, and the sun was setting on the tip of the ocean. Willow yawned and told Silver and Landon they could clean up. She was tired and was going to bed. But before she could walk through the French doors, Landon got up and walked inside with her.

He looked at Willow severely and said, "You need to know Mom is having her checkup soon. I'm going to go with her. I'll let you know how things are looking." Willow nodded and hugged her brother. Every time for the last 10 years that their mom had to go back to the oncologist for checkups, the entire family walked on eggshells. Willow knew Landon would handle everything and if anything were amiss, he would call her.

She kissed him on the cheek and said call me and let me know. "If I need to go down early, I can, Willow told her big brother. "Oh and by the way, this vacation "situation" here, I was a bit upset at first, but we have more important things to worry about than Silver Bleu."

Landon walked outside to tell Silver goodbye and to inform Silver he would be returning to work to handle some administration matters. He told Silver to stay in touch and not be a stranger.

Silver sat outside by himself for a while. He knew something was up with Landon and Willow. He had left them alone so they could talk. He heard Landon's car pull away and Willow lock the front door. After a few moments, he knew she had gone into her bedroom.

Silver wanted to tell her what a great job she had done with dinner tonight but did not want to disturb her if she were asleep. He walked back in and locked up behind him. As he walked past Willow's room, he saw her undressing. She was putting her pajamas on. Her top was just coming down over her head. He could see the curve of her breasts and her petite nipples as the shirt slid down over them. Willow only had her bikini panties on, and just as Silver had imagined, the cheeks of that cute derriere were muscular and round. He could tell they would fit nicely in the palm of his hands. How he long just to squeeze them. Before he could catch himself and walk away, Willow looked at him. It was not a look of startlement, but one of anticipation.

Should he move forward or should he apologize for staring? Silver did not have to decide. Willow started walking towards him. Silver felt the room rise in temperature. It was as if the room were two degrees hotter.

Silver smiled as Willow moved into his embrace, like she belonged there. He heard her say, "I just need a hug," she whispered. "That's all, Silver. I just need a hug."

Silver obliged without any hesitation. "Whatever it is, Willow, all will be well." He felt her quiet breath against his chest as she thanked him. Lord, Silver did not want to let go of her and embrace. She fit rather nicely in his arms, like a missing piece of a puzzle.

"Silver..." Willow started.

"Yes, sweetheart? Silver replied.

"I can't breathe. I'm going to pass out. You got to let go a bit." This was good. Willow did not want him to let her go. He gently let go but kept her body within his embrace and protection.

"Is there anything that I can do? Tell me what is going on. Is it your mom?" Willow knew she would need to tell Silver what she and Landon had discussed. Willow would be leaving tonight to go see her parents in Blessings. Landon had told Willow their dad needed help in taking care of mom, and if she could arrive before him, it would be a tremendous help. Willow knew Landon would not be able to get away from work as quickly, and with her being self-employed, she was able to do things at the drop of a hat. The hat was definitely dropping.

Willow turned her cheek to lay on Silver's strong shoulder. "No. I will be packing and leaving tonight. Landon asked if I could help our dad with a few matters with Mom."

Silver pulled gently at her shoulders to lean her back and said, "I'll drive you to the airport." Willow knew if he did this, she would not be able to hold the tears back. So far, she was doing a pretty good job of maintaining some type of control. She told him no. When she returned, she would need her car to bring her back to Landon's.

"Nonsense," Silver told her. "No need to pay the fee for overnight parking. Go pack whatever you need. Get changed into your travel clothes. Get the flight confirmed, and we will head out."

CHAPTER 19

Silver listened as Willow made the arrangements for the flight. Lord, he remembered so much about their farm and how much he enjoyed the country and the simplicity of not being rushed to any and everything.

Willow walked out with her small luggage bag. She did not want to have to wait to have everything tagged. She had placed as much as she could inside, wanting to only have the one carry-on.

Willow walked to the door with Silver following behind her. "Go ahead," he said. "I'll lock everything up. The rental car is unlocked." Silver noticed the small drop of her shoulders. She had had the weight of the world placed upon her in less than 30 minutes.

He walked to the car. Willow had already buckled herself in. She was reviewing her phone for the flight. Silver began the drive to the airport. The entire drive was silent as he knew Willow had a lot on her mind.

When Silver pulled up to the airport, he put the flashers on and walked around to open Willow's door. Silver walked with her to the check-in. Before she could walk away through the sliding glass doors, he turned Willow towards him and kissed her. He did not know why he had chosen this moment. It just felt as if he should reassure her that he was going to be here when she returned.

Willow did not want the kiss to end. She did not know how or why Silver had started the kiss, but it made her feel very warm, from head to toe. Silver could feel the change in Willow. She opened her lips slightly, allowing him access to her taste. She could not help but take a small inhale of breath between the kiss. Silver pulled her closer to him. Willow did not want to leave his embrace. Silver did not know how long the kiss had lasted, but it ended too soon.

"Silver," Willow said as she at last pulled away from Silver's lips. "I have to leave or I'll miss the flight." Silver nodded.

With one last hug and kiss to her forehead, he looked at Willow and said, "Call me when you land. Let me know how things look. Let me know when you return, and I will be here waiting." Willow almost let that one tear trickle, but she knew if one started, it would be like a waterfall taking place again. She gave one last hug to Silver and walked into the airport. She knew she did not need to turn around. Willow felt his eyes on her, but she had to know. Just before she walked through the doors, she turned for one last look at him. He *was* watching her. He waved. Willow waved back. And then walked through the doors to catch her flight.

Silver pulled back into the driveway. As he entered the house, he knew he needed to prepare the presentation for the next day of the medical conference. He went to his bedroom, pulled out his research documents, placed them on the bed, and set his laptop up to review his power point. There were a few areas that still need tweaking. Needing a distraction, Silver began to work diligently. Before he knew it, the sun had begun to lower. Silver looked at the time. It was already past seven. He needed to stretch and move. He went to the kitchen and grabbed a bottled water from the refrigerator. He walked out to the deck and decided to take the path to the beach.

As Silver walked the beach, he could feel where the sun had kissed the sand on his bare feet. It really was not as hot as he had thought it would be. Just a bit toasty. He allowed his thoughts to reflect on the day's events and that kiss. It had not been planned but the reaction was even more surprising to Silver. He admitted to himself that there was something between him and Willow. He had felt it and he knew she had, too. Silver turned back to the house and wondered if she had landed yet. Willow had promised she would call, and she should have landed by now. Silver was praying that everything was okay.

CHAPTER 20

Willow boarded the plane with only thoughts of that kiss swimming in her head. What in the world had just happened? Why in the world had she responded? What would happen when she returned? They would have to discuss it. Willow brought her fingers to her mouth and slowly rubbed them across her lips. Lips that were swollen with passion. Lips that had been kissed by her brother's best friend.

The entire flight, Willow tried to occupy her time with small things. When the flight attendant came around with snacks, she accepted a small snack since she did not know if she would be going straight to her parents' home or to the hospital. This part, she had not relayed to Silver. There just had not been enough time. As the plane began its descent into the airport, Willow remembered she had promised to call Silver once she landed.

Willow called her father once she had landed and hailed a taxi. Her father informed her that they were home. Her mom had been released and they were both excited to see her. Willow felt herself let out the breath she had been holding. Her mother was the glue that held the family together. After she hung up with her father, Willow knew she needed to call Silver, but she wanted to see her mom first.

The taxicab driver pulled into her parents' driveway. Home. She was home. Willow and Landon had grown up in this log cabin. It was not fancy nor expensive. There were no emotions nor feelings that can describe what it felt like to finally be home after being away for any length of time. Willow paid, thanked the driver and grabbed her carry on.

As soon as the door shut to the taxi, Willow looked up and saw her dad standing in the doorway smiling with his arms opened wide. "Well come on in, baby girl!" he called happily. Willow could not resist. She slung her carry on to the ground and ran as fast as she could. Hugs were the best. Hugs could fix any bad day. Willow's dad held her tight and whispered, "I am so glad you're home. She's missed you." Willow did not know what to expect when she walked in. But she was pleasantly surprised. Her mom was in the kitchen cooking something that was smelling the entire house with the aroma of bacon and biscuits. Willow knew exactly what her mom was cooking for supper –breakfast. As she walked into the kitchen, Willow saw that her mom had made what she had been dreaming of the entire flight. Bacon, eggs, biscuits, gravy, and fried potatoes.

Willow walked up behind her mom and leaned over her shoulder and inhaled the wonderful smell of breakfast. Her mother grinned from ear to ear. "When I found out you were coming home, I had to make your favorite meal," her mom commented. Nothing could be better. Willow was home.

The sun was setting. Willow tried to hide her yawn, but her mother saw right through it. "You're tired honey. Let's eat and then head to bed, and we will talk in the morning. I am not going anywhere and neither are you." Willow hated to admit it, but getting in her pajamas and laying under the blankets that had been hand sewn by her mother was all she needed. The family ate supper together. The only person or persons missing were Landon and Silver. When Willow finished, she did as her mom had instructed her.

Her room was still hers. There was pink and blue country gingham accents scattered throughout her room. Her sleigh bed was calling her name. Willow hoped that Silver would understand why she had not returned his call. She was just so exhausted.

CHAPTER 21

How long had the flight taken? Had she landed yet? Was she okay? Did she catch a cab? Had she even thought about transportation? Silver could not believe he was asking himself all these questions about Willow. He was worried about her. He remembered the pain Landon and Willow had gone through when their mom had been diagnosed. As a friend, he had felt helpless. Silver had offered words of encouragement and his time to his friend, but it never felt good enough. But, why had Willow not called yet?

Silver needed something to do other than to think about Willow and if she was okay. He decided that he would take another walk on the beach to calm his nerves, or least attempt to soothe his worries.

After an unsuccessful walk, he finally decided to call it a night. He had to get up early in the morning in order to make sure his handouts were ready for the attendees of the conference. Sometimes the small things like that made the biggest impact. Silver was sure more than 50 percent of the attendees would probably place them in the waste basket on their way out from the conference, but there were the other 50 percent who might keep them in a binder for future reference. He was worried he had not heard from Willow, but ultimately decided no news was good news. Silver laid down in the quiet of Landon's home. It felt weird not having Willow near him and the knowledge that she was just in the other room. Silver hoped she would call.

The morning started off with the most incredible smell of breakfast and coffee brewing. Willow did not like coffee, but she knew it was a morning ritual for her dad. Before heading to work, he would grab a cup of coffee and head to the porch to read the Bible. Willow and Landon knew this was the time their father needed to begin his day. It was not a bad way to begin. Coffee, meditation, and prayer. She knew when she walked in the kitchen and did not see him that he would be where she remembered. Even as a young woman, Willow had never wanted to disturb his time with God.

She walked into the kitchen. She inhaled the aroma of the biscuits her mom was bringing out of the oven. "Good morning," her mother said."

"Good morning, Mom. How are you feeling?"

Willow's mother touched her gently on the arm. "I am fine. It was just one of those kinda days that puts family in an alert mode. I think it affected your father more so than me." Willow could see that. Willow knew how in love her parents were. They had been married for more than 30 years. There had been ups and downs, but more ups than downs.

"How have you been doing, Willow? Anyone of interest in your life you need to tell me about?" Willow's thoughts immediately turned to Silver. His face appeared in her mind as she remembered how they had met in the driveway while she was trying to unload all her luggage. He had just stood there. She could not help the smile that came to her face, and Willow's mother caught the emotion. "Well, tell me about him, Willow."

Willow suddenly remembered she had promised him. "Mom, excuse me," she said. "I have to make call." Willow walked back into her bedroom and dialed Silver's number.

Several rings passed before she heard "Hello, can I help you? This is Dr. Silver Bleu."

Willow laughed. "I do not know if you can help me, but for the moment, I am okay. It's Willow."

She heard him inhale for a brief second and then him say, "Thank goodness. You had me worried for a bit. I'm in the middle of my conference, Willow. Can I call you back?" Willow had forgotten about his conference.

"Yes, Silver! I am so sorry. I did not look at my clock when I called. Whenever it's convenient for you." She heard Silver chuckle with his deep, husky voice.

"I wish now was convenient, but I can't. I'll call you later. I promise." And with that, Silver had hung up.

Willow walked back into the kitchen to see both her parents were at the table and ready to eat. Willow sat down, and her dad reached out to grab her hand to begin prayer. Willow looked at her parents. They were aging. Both she and Landon had spoken about what would happen to the farm, if their parents were unable to maintain its upkeep. But for this moment, Willow would not allow herself to think about that. She was going to enjoy being home.

Silver finished his presentation in record-timing. As he was packing up the left-over materials from the day, a female hand stopped him with an offer to help. He turned to see who the hand belonged to. It was one of the assistants who had been assigned to help Silver during his stay. Silver made small talk with her as they cleaned up. At first, he thought she was one of the new interns. She laughed and had told him no. She had told him her name was Evergreen. Silver thought it was an unusual name, but it fit her. She had long straight blonde hair and big blue eyes. She seemed a few years younger than Silver. She had politely told him she was working part-time to help pay for studio time, for she was a country music artist. She was very pleasant and easy to talk to. It took Silver's mind off the fact that he had not had a chance to call Willow back as he promised. Once they were done, he thanked Evergreen for her help and wished her luck on her dreams. Silver had a feeling that this young lady would succeed in whatever she put her mind to.

Silver got in his car and drove back to Landon's home. He felt uneasy, but could not put his finger on why. As he approached the house, Silver decided to call Willow. The phone rang and rang but there was no answer. Silver had never been known for his patience. He had none. When he wanted something done, he did it himself. He did not have time to wait for someone else to make a decision. The unanswered call was too suspicious for Silver to let go. He immediately texted Landon to be sure he had the address of Landon's and Willow's home correct. After he had confirmation, he texted Willow he would see her soon. Before he could second guess himself, Silver booked a flight to Blessings, Wyoming.

CHAPTER 22

Silver landed around midnight. He had rented an SVU to get him to the farm. Once he was on his way to the farm, Silver felt a bit more at ease. He just needed to see her in person. He just needed to touch her. He just – what *did* he just need to do? Silver questioned himself. They had only been together for a few short days, but Silver knew something had taken place. He could not believe he was traipsing all over God's earth for a woman. Hell would probably freeze over. As Silver pulled down the rocky road that led to the farm, he had texted Willow to let her know he would be arriving.

Willow could not believe he was flying to Blessings. She giggled to herself because that was what one did when someone does what Silver was doing – flying halfway across the States, just to check on her. She had told her mom and dad that she would be staying up late, but she had not told them why. Willow was sitting in the den, perusing through several interior design books when she saw the lights coming down the road. Her heart skipped a beat. She suddenly felt as if she could not breathe. He would be here any moment. Silver would be walking through the door – her home. Get it together, Willow she thought to herself.

Silver stopped the SVU and turned the lights out and walked briskly to the front porch. Lord, it had not changed. It was still as welcoming as it had been when he had been in college. As he was about to text Willow to let her know he was outside, the door opened and he heard her voice, "Well, a bit late for a house call, don't you think, Dr. Silver Bleu? What brings you to Blessings?"

Without any thought, without any hesitation, without any caution to the wind, Silver leaned into Willow, whispered, "you do," and lowered his mouth to Willow's.

Willow knew, when Silver leaned in, what was going to happen. She knew by the fluttering in her stomach and the rapid beating of her heart, Silver was going to do what Willow had been unable to get out of her mind since the airport.

It was like floating outside her body. Silver kissed Willow with such intensity. His tongue demanded Willow respond, and respond she did. She could not help it; she leaned into Silver. Her gasping breaths told Silver that Willow was enjoying the kiss. The swelling of her lips indicated Willow felt as passionate as Silver did.

He could not resist any longer. He could not resist what he had known for a while. He was attracted to Willow. He knew Willow felt the same. He could see it in the taut nipples of her small, rounded breasts that were showing through her tight pajama top.

He looked deeply into Willow's eyes. "Look at me," he said. "Did you not think I would find out how you felt? Did you not think the truth would reveal itself? Did you not think that this would happen?" Willow could not breathe. Deep in her heart, she knew she could not stop what was about to happen.

Willow looked at Silver and said, "It will not happen because I will not allow it. I cannot allow it."

Silver laughed heartily. "It will happen and you will ask for more."

"Never."

"Never is a long time, Willow." Silver grinned.

CHAPTER 23

"This is going to happen tonight. It can happen right here on the front porch of your mom and dad's house, or it can happen inside the warmth of their home. You choose," Silver stated as matter-of-factly.

Willow just shook her head. "I don't know what to do," she told Silver.

Silver put his hand under her chin and said, "I do. Trust me."

Silver gently took Willow's hand, opened the door, and quietly led them through the house. They stopped in the living room. Silver began kissing Willow at the top of her forehead. He moved to the tip of her nose, then to her earlobes, then her neck. Willow was melting. She was melting like butter on popcorn. Willow no longer had the strength to deny what she had wanted all along. She wanted and needed Silver. She needed to be held within the safety of his arms. She felt Silver stop kissing her. She lifted her head to see the desire in Silver's eyes. The color of his eyes, as he stared back, were so intense. She could feel the same intense desire pressing against her innermost being.

Silver knew Willow was feeling the same as him. The room was steadily becoming hotter. He needed to get out of the constricting clothes.

Silver needed to feel Willow against him. "If I begin— like I want to do, Willow, and I think you do, too—I cannot be responsible for stopping myself. When I see you you staring at me like you are right now, I am smitten." Willow smiled. Her mom and dad had used that word about their relationship and marriage. She nodded her head in agreement. She felt like she had just made a decision that would determine her future. Before she could deny the magnetism she had with Silver, she took his hand and walked towards her bedroom.

She placed her two small fingers to her lips and whispered, "Sssshhh. I don't want to wake Mom and Dad". Silver chuckled. He followed Willow into her bedroom. He watched as she turned around, ever so slowly. He could see her anticipation through her body language. He shut her bedroom door quietly and turned the locked.

Silver walked towards Willow. "This night, Willow, I promise you will never forget. Come here." Without any thought, Willow walked until she was standing right in front of Silver. He encircled her in his arms and moved his hands to gently cup her breasts, rubbing from the outside of her shirt. Her nipples became taut until Silver could see her need for him. He continued his caressing.

"Remember, Willow, if you want me to stop, then please say so."

Willow whispered the words Silver had longed to hear his entire trip here, "No, I do not want you to stop."

With the ease and movement of a feather, Silver unbuttoned her soft, silky top. He slid one shoulder off. Silver kissed that shoulder lovingly. He slowly slid the other side of the top off until the only thing between Willow and Silver was her lacy bra.

He placed his hands on each of Willow's bra straps and slid one finger underneath, slowly sliding each strap down her arms. Silver watched her breasts rise as she inhaled sharply, and he knew Willow desired him. He reached around Willow's back and swiftly undid her bra, and it fell to the floor. Willow moved both her hands to cover her breasts.

"Don't," Silver told her. "I just need you to stand there so I can admire your natural beauty." Willow had never in her life felt so helpless and vulnerable, but at the same time, so aroused. These were feelings Willow had always pushed away.

CHAPTER 24

Willow had learned early on she was quite picky when it came to men. She compared most to her mom and dad and the love that she had seen them share. She also was hit rather hard with the conclusion that most men did not understand her desire to continue her work. Willow had never allowed herself time for romance.

She was cautious when it came to love. Standing in front of Silver, baring her soul to him, had not been in Willow's plans. Though, if she was honest with herself, she did not ever want to move from his stare.

Silver noticed that a small frown had formed on Willow's face. Silver leaned forward, and whispered, "A penny for your thoughts."

Willow smiled. "Dr. Silver Bleu, you don't want to know. I am afraid I may shock you." Silver grinned. At least she did not back away from him.

"If you tell me what you're thinking, I'll tell you what I'm thinking," Silver teased.

Willow looked at him with desire in her eyes. "I cannot believe I am standing here in front of you, Silver, baring more than my soul. I am baring my heart. I cannot believe this moment is happening. And I don't want to you to get a big head, but I have dreamed of you kissing me since the moment Landon introduced you to our family. Now, tell me what you are thinking," Willow looked at him expectantly.

Silver said, in a deep, husky voice, "A promise is a promise. The day I pulled into the driveway and saw the silhouette of your body from your car, I knew there was something familiar about you. When you turned around, I could not believe it. And here you are in front of me, and I still cannot believe it. If you want me to stop right here, right now, I will. I'll sleep on the couch."

Before Silver could finish the last sentence, Willow dropped her hands from her breast and placed both her hands on Silver's strong chest and shook her head no.

Silver watched as she did this. She was gorgeous. He took Willow's hands in his. "I just want to kiss you. Kiss you like you have never been kissed before. Kiss you until you cannot breathe. Kiss you until you beg me for more."

Before Willow could say anything, Silver leaned in and nibbled at the lobe of Willow's ear. A shiver went through her. Silver kissed his way down the side of her neck with small, suckling kisses until he reached the roundness of her breasts. He swirled his tongue around her nipple, then gently suckled until he heard Willow gasp. With his free hand, he took the nipple of her other breast between his thumb and finger, gently circling around the areola until the nipple became swollen with desire.

His touch was sending her into the heavens. Willow felt like she would fall were it not for Silver's muscular chest holding her up. When he heard her moan of satisfaction, he kissed a path back to her swollen lips. He tugged at her bottom lip with his teeth, forcing her to open her mouth. He wanted to kiss Willow not just tenderly, but thoroughly.

Willow opened her lips and felt Silver slide his tongue inside. The kiss was filled with passion and purpose. It had become a need for Willow. She needed all of Silver. Not just the touching or the kissing. She needed what she knew awaited.

CHAPTER 25

Silver knew when the direction of the kiss changed. He realized that he wanted more from Willow. The kissing was flirtatious and teasing, but he required more.

He looked into her eyes and saw the desire written there. He pulled his lips away and gently slid his hand inside Willow's pajama bottoms. He cupped her buttocks and pulled her close to him so she could feel the intensity of his need. He heard her intake of her breath. "Willow, I cannot stop. Do not ask me to stop. Tell me what you want. Tell me where to touch you. Tell me your deepest desire," he whispered. Willow had never been asked such questions. All she could think of was her need to have Silver inside of her. She needed to feel the rhythm of two bodies joined together as one.

Willow had barely noticed she was no longer wearing her bottoms. How had they fallen to the floor without her noticing? Her entire soul and being was bare. It was as if she were caught in a dream and did not want to wake. She knew Silver was waiting for an answer. She reached for Silver and began to palm his manhood through his pants. Silver was already hard. It did not take long for Willow to realize Silver wanted her as much as she needed him. Willow unbuckled his belt and unzipped his pants. Before she could lose her nerve, she placed her hand to feel his bare skin.

She felt him breathe deeply and heard him say, "Careful, there is nothing but danger there, and you're playing with fire." Willow did not care. She was already hot. Her entire being was burning for Silver's touch.

Silver trailed another path of feathery kisses from her ear lobe to the peak of her breasts. Silver took the tip of her nipple and gently caressed it with his tongue. Willow arched her back to allow him easier access.

Silver backed Willow up until she hit the edge of her bed. With one arm, he scooped her and laid her gently on her bed. Silver took Willow's hands high above her head and intertwined his fingers through hers. He felt Willow part her legs for him. He took his manhood and began swirling motions on the outer edge of her clitoris until he felt Willow's body relax. She did not know how much longer she could wait for Silver. The warmth, the moisture, the ache of needing him was too much.

Willow heard him say, "I cannot hold back any longer." With one thrust he was inside of Willow. Silver did not know if Willow was experienced in lovemaking, but he could only determine that her body was reacting to him because of a need. A need he intended to fulfill.

Instinct gave way as her body arched to meet his teasing thrusts. She moved in perfect time with Silver.

"Willow look at me. I want to see that you desire me as much as I desire you." Willow opened her eyes. Silver knew things had changed between them. They could never go back to just being friends. Silver knew in his heart that this beautiful young lady was about to change his life forever.

Silver could feel her clitoris react to him. She was moist to his manhood. Silver felt Willow's legs wrap tightly around his waist to pull him deeper inside her. He would only be able to hold on to self-control for just a few more minutes. Willow cupped both her hands around his buttocks. She didn't need to pull him forward. Silver knew the need and knew the outcome would be explosive. Silver leaned down to kiss Willow, and then his last ounce of control shred as he thrust himself inside Willow's warmth and held her body tight. Willow raised her body to match the intensity of his thrust until she was utterly spent from satisfaction. She knew when Silver reached his point of release. He stayed inside of her, making small, teasing pushes to escalate Willow's craving for his touch.

As her heart stopped racing, Willow opened her eyes to see Silver staring intensely at her forehead. Had she done something wrong? Had he not enjoyed himself? She moved slightly, and Silver looked into her eyes. "Go to sleep pretty girl. I'm not going anywhere." Before she could say anything, Silver grabbed a blanket from the floor and placed it over both of them. The heat of Silver's body and the excitement of what had just transpired between them made Willow very sleepy. She wondered how her mother and father would react to her having a man in her room, especially when they realized it was Silver, as she began to drift off to sleep. She smiled to herself. She had felt the true act and emotion of love. But was she in love with Silver or was it just pure sexual attraction? She could not think any more. She was tired from their lovemaking. Willow fell asleep with Silver's hand on her waist and the security that he would be there when she woke up. As she moved closer to Silver, he pulled her deep within the safety of his being.

CHAPTER 26

There was a knock on the bedroom door. Willow heard it but could not bring herself completely awake. She felt the weight of something across her stomach. She tried to roll, but as she did, the hand cupping her breast pulled her closer. She heard a familiar voice whisper in her ear, "Don't move, I want to hold you just a bit longer." The evening's affair all came crashing back to Willow. She turned on her back to see Silver. He moved his hand to play with her bared breast. He gently tugged at her nipple. The knock came again, this time more insistent and panicky than the first.

Then Willow heard her mother's voice ask, "Willow, honey, are you okay in there?" Willow grabbed Silver's hands and told him to behave.

He chuckled softly, so Willow's mother could not hear, and then looked attentively at Willow. "I'll behave, but only until tonight."

Willow knew she could not argue with Silver. Both were nude. Her mother's knocking became more insistent, and Willow knew she would have to open the door quickly or her mother would bust it down. Willow pulled away from Silver's touch and placed her hands to lips to quiet Silver. She moved to the side of the bed and reached to grab her sweats laying on the floor. "Sssshhh, I have to break it to Mom and Dad gently that a man is in here with me, and I have to prepare them that it is their son's best friend from college."

Silver laughed heartily. "Go right ahead, Willow. I want to hear your explanation, as well. I'll go jump in the shower, while you try to make a plausible excuse as to why there is a naked man in your bed." Before Willow could respond, Silver pulled the blanket off the bed, wrapped it tightly around his muscular body, walked to the door, and opened it. He greeted Willow's parents with, "Good morning Mr. and Mrs. Dawson. It is a beautiful morning." He turned, looked at Willow, and winked.

Willow could not believe that Silver had just done what she had hoped he would not. She was doomed, and there would be a thousand questions, now.

As Silver walked past Willow's mother, Willow's mom looked at Silver and then at Willow. "Young lady, you have some explaining to do, and it will not wait." Willow nodded her head in agreement.

She kissed her dad on the cheek as she walked past him with a small greeting. He commented with a chuckle, "You're on your own, little lady." Willow loved her dad very much. He had a compassionate heart. She was a daddy's girl.

"Geeze, thanks dad. Throwing me to the lions, aren't ya?"

Her dad just replied, "Whatever she asks, just tell her the truth."

As Willow followed her mother into the kitchen, Willow started with, "Mom, I can explain," but before she could utter another word, the doorbell rang. Willow's mother turned towards her and asked if she would answer it.

Willow walked towards the door, and in doing so, overheard Silver singing in the shower. Lord, she was getting off track. The door, someone was at the door. It was too early to be handling so much.

Willow opened the door and, standing there smiling like a Cheshire cat, was Landon. "Oh, baby sister," he complained, "you didn't, did you? No, don't answer that. I already knew when I did not find him at the house. He's here, isn't he?"

"Well, the entire world knows now, evidently," Willow stated. "Come on in. Mom wants an explanation, and I guess you do, too."

Landon hugged her and told her, "No, you are a grown woman. You make your own bed and lie in it."

They turned to walk inside together and that was the just as Silver was exiting the bathroom. They all stood there in the living room looking at one another. Willow could not help herself. She began to giggle and could not stop. Before anyone could say anything, Willow explained Silver had flown and then drove the rest of the way to the house. He had gotten in late last night, and Willow had not wanted to wake anyone. So, Silver had shared her room.

Without one word, Willow's mom and dad looked at each other and said, "What's for breakfast?" Landon looked at Silver and nodded his head towards Landon's room, telling Silver he wanted to talk.

CHAPTER 27

Landon closed the door behind them and immediately, with a stern voice, told Silver he was not happy. "Don't hurt her. Don't play with her feelings, Silver. She may just be a conquest or "another notch in your belt", but I'm telling you stay away from my baby sister."

Silver did not know whether to laugh or to be mad he had just been told to stay away from Willow, who was old enough to make her own decisions, and based on last night's events, knew exactly what she wanted in a man.

Before Silver could reply, Landon continued "I know how you operate. Remember, we have been friends for quite some time, and I have seen lot of adventures and broken hearts along the way."

Silver smiled. "I know, Landon. I remember our college years. I also remember seeing Willow when we would return here. But I also know she is not a little girl anymore."

"You are correct. She is not a little girl anymore, but she also is not going to have her heart broken by you. She is still my sister. And I won't allow it. She has a lot going on with her career. We have Mom to take care of. Right now, it is just not good timing for your usual one-night stand. I think it would be best if you leave today. I can tell Willow you needed to return to my home to finalize some conference matters. Sound good to you?".

"Okay. Sounds good to me," Silver answered. "Actually, no, it doesn't sound good to me. I really do like Willow. And frankly, Landon, it's none of your business if I'm in a relationship with your sister or not."

Silver looked at Landon, and he knew Landon was serious. When it came to family, Landon and his sister were tighter than thieves. Silver valued the bond he and Landon shared as brothers. Silver did not want to hurt Willow, but in doing so, Silver knew his and Landon's relationship would be damaged. He did not want to upset either Willow or Landon, but it seemed like one would end up hurt no matter what.

Silver nodded his head in acknowledgement of Landon's concern about Willow. "I'll leave today," Silver said.

Landon looked at Silver. "I think it's best for all. No hard feelings. I'll see you back at my house in Florida."

Silver opened the door and walked into the bedroom where he had made love to Willow. Willow was in the kitchen with her parents, allowing Silver time to get dressed. She had noticed that Landon and Silver had been in Landon's bedroom with the door closed for quite some time. She had overheard some tense moments but did not think anything about it until she heard Landon's door open and saw Silver walk into her bedroom. Willow knew better than to leave the table to investigate, though. Landon came in and sat down beside her. She looked at Landon. "Everything okay?"

"Absolutely," he said.

Breakfast was coming to an end, so Willow helped her mom clean up. In doing so, Willow did not hear Silver's footsteps along the hardwood living room floor. She turned around just in time to see Silver with his bag over his shoulder. He was shaking her dad's hand and hugging her mom. What was going on? Where was Silver going?

Before she could walk towards Silver, Landon came up behind up her and said, "It's for your best interest, little sister." She watched Silver walk out the front door. What had happened? What had Landon done? She drove her elbow into Landon's stomach.

"I'll never forgive you," she cried.

Willow ran out the front door in time to see Silver's truck pulling down the driveway. Where was he going? Would she ever see him again? Slowly, the tears began to fall down her cheeks. She could not stop the them from flowing. He had left her. He had not even given her an explanation. He had not even told her goodbye. What had she done so wrong? Would she ever know why Silver had left?

Willow turned and walked back into her parents' home. She had not wiped the tears away. She looked at Landon and pointed her finger at him and asked, "What did you say to Silver?"

Landon knew he had to tell her the truth. He knew Silver. He had known Silver almost as long as his little sister, Willow. This was the best thing for all. So, Landon told Willow the conversation he had had with Silver held in Landon's bedroom.

After listening to him, Willow could not look at Landon. She could not believe Landon had told Silver to leave. She could not believe her brother was still trying to control her life. She was so upset with Landon. Willow did not want to talk to Landon, or even see him. She told Landon that she was quite capable of taking care of their mom and dad, so he should just leave and return home. Landon tried to object, but Willow cut him off. "Really? You are going to tell me how to live my life, but won't let me take care of our parents alone? Careful, Landon. Remember, I know your secret. I know you still pine for her. I know you still think about Evergreen. So, let's just say, I won't interfere in your love life if you don't interfere in mine. I figure that's a fair trade."

Landon just stood there. In shock or dismay, he did not know which, but his baby sister was no longer a baby. She was a beautiful young woman who knew what she wanted and was not afraid to tell him. He admired her for this because he still had not admitted it to himself, he was in love with Evergreen. He had never not loved Evergreen.

Willow was watching Landon. She knew what he was thinking and knew what needed to be done. She walked towards her big brother and wrapped her arms around him. "I tell you what, Landon. If you go after your true love, so will I. Let's get Mom taken care of, help dad around the house, and take it from there. Deal?"

Landon smiled at his baby sister and said, "I know you have found your love. Truly Willow, I could not have wished for a better man than Silver to sweep you off your feet.

Willow said, "Oh. big brother, let's get mom taken care of, and let's go find our hearts."

CHAPTER 28

As Silver had left Willow behind at her parents', he had looked in the rearview mirror. He had seen Willow run out the door. He had seen Willow standing there all alone. He knew he had hurt Willow. What had he done?

There's an old saying, "time heals all wounds." Silver did not believe this. He had returned to Landon's home in Florida. The entire flight back had been consumed with the last image he had of Willow in his mind – her standing alone in her parents' driveway. Silver had returned to Star Bright Hospital to do a final meeting with the doctors. He had enjoyed talking with the other pediatricians, especially the doctors who specialized in cancer research.

Silver knew his time in Shadow Creek was limited, and he knew he would have to return to Pioneer Children's Hospital and back to his responsibilities eventually. He had attempted to call Willow several times while still at Landon's house. All the calls went to voice mail. Landon had told him Willow had been busy helping take care of their parents and opening her new business in Blessings. Silver knew Landon was upset with him, and Landon, out of sibling protection, would only give Silver tidbits of what was taking place with Willow.

As Silver was packing and loading his truck to head back to the airport, Silver could not help but think back to the first day he had seen Willow and her determination while unloading all her luggage. It brought a smile to his face. Silver hated to admit it, but Willow had left Silver wanting something he had not thought he would ever need or want, the need for a relationship… with her.

Silver double checked Landon's home to be sure he had not left anything of his own and that the house was in clean condition. He walked through the door, turned around and locked it. As he opened his truck door, he turned one last time to look back at the house where his destiny had changed. The place that would forever be etched in his memory.

CHAPTER 29

Silver pulled into Pioneer Children's Hospital parking lot. He had returned late Sunday night. Mondays were always difficult. The New Year would soon be arriving. As Silver opened the truck door to begin the day, he could not help but wonder about Willow. I wonder if she thinks of that night, he asked himself. Silver needed to get back into his routine. Sometimes routine was good. Silver needed Pioneer's and Pioneer's needed him. It was a haven, and it was a place to hide. Silver knew there was much to share with the staff, and he knew they would plunge head-first into the new adventures he had learned while away. There were many new exciting techniques and medicines to discuss with the Pediatric Oncology Department. Familiarity is what Silver needed. So, began his first day back. All memories of Willow Rainey Dawson locked away.

It was not an easy few weeks, but Willow was able to attend all the follow-up medical appointments for their mom. Landon had decided to return to his home. She knew Landon had wanted to check in on his friend.

All their mother's test results came back negative. Both Willow and Landon felt blessed. Their dad was elated and relieved. Willow knew that their family needed a bit of respite from all the worrying they had been doing.

Willow could hear her mother in the kitchen. She was humming to herself. It was a sound so beautiful to Willow. She sat on the edge of the bed and looked up. She thanked God for His mercy and grace. She remained there for quite a spell. She did not know how long. When she looked up, she saw her dad peering through the door.

"You okay, pumpkin?" he asked Willow.

"I am, Dad. Just saying a few prayers," Willow smiled at him.

"Me too, baby girl. Me too." He walked in and sat on the edge of the bed with Willow. "I know you need to get back, and get back to being you and tie matters up. Your mom and I appreciate all that you have done. We know it's time. We are excited that you will be opening your business in Blessings and realize loose ends need to be finalized. We also know that you miss him." Willow laughed. She could never hide her emotions or feelings from her dad. He always knew when something was wrong. He always had the best advice.

"Thank you, Daddy. I do need to get back to work and home so I can begin the move." Her dad placed his arm around her shoulder and pulled her close and whispered, "You need him, too. Let me know when you are packed and arrangements are made for the flight back. Both your mom and I will take you."

CHAPTER 30

Willow walked into the kitchen to tell her mother goodbye. She wrapped her arms around her mom's waist from behind and leaned her chin on her mother's small shoulder. "Mom, please tell me its going to be all right."

Willow's mom patted Willow's hand and said, "Of course. Why wouldn't it? I've got your dad, you, and Landon, and the Good Lord, plus you are going to open your business here. Big adventures."

What more do I need?" Willow kissed her mom goodbye and took one last look at what she considered to be her first, true love – the home that her parents had built on faith, love, and trust.

Willow and her dad drove into the airport. Like a gentleman, her dad opened her door for her when they arrived. Willow grabbed her small carry on. She immediately fell into her dad's strong hug. "I know you already know that I know," he began and Willow began to laugh.

"Yes, daddy, I already know that you know."

"Listen to your heart, Willow. Listen to what God whispers. Just listen."

A small tear fell from the corner of Willow's eyes. "I will, Daddy. I promise."

As her plane landed, Willow had no idea what she was going to do next. She had told her dad that she would not be flying back to Landon's home. She knew for a fact Landon would not be there, and with as much time that had passed, Willow was pretty sure that Silver had returned to Pioneer Children's Hospital. The entire flight she wondered what Silver was doing. Had he returned to his normal routine at Pioneer's? Had he given one thought to Willow? Had he thought about anything that one night? So many questions. So many questions unanswered.

Willow drove her car up in the drive to her small country log cabin home – the perks of working for one of the top interior log cabin design companies. She loved her job and was looking forward to returning to work. She had the whole weekend to mull the last few weeks over and move on. She had to begin preparing for the move of her interior design business to Blessings in order to be closer to her mom and dad. Something told Willow this "mulling thing" was not going to be easy. She missed his teasing. She missed his smile. She genuinely missed him and how she felt when she was around him. A euphoria like none she had ever experienced before. It was natural. It was plain and simple, Willow loved him. She could not deny it any longer. Willow had always known. Even when she was younger and had fantasized about Silver Bleu, she had known he was the one. Willow wondered if Silver felt the same

Silver threw himself into his work. His co-workers had commented that he had become quieter upon his return. Several had commented to Dr. Chrystmas they thought Silver was coming down with something. Nick knew what the "something" was. The something was Landon's little sister, Willow Rainey Dawson. Nick had felt the same way when he thought he had lost Winter.

94

He laughed as Silver walked through the cafeteria line and was polite and smiled to everyone, but Nick knew. As John Wayne said: "A goal, a love, and a dream give you total control over your body and your life." Silver's goal, love, and dream was wrapped in a petite female body by the name of Willow. Nick was going to have to help his dear friend realize this, or else the entire hospital staff was going to need to help, for even they knew he had fallen in love. They just did not know with whom. Yet.

As Silver approached a table to set his tray down, Nick asked, "Did you call her, did you text her, did you do anything, Silver, to help your cause? Any more days of you sulking around here with those big, sad, puppy-dog eyes and the staff is going to make the call for you."

Silver looked at his best friend. "No, I have not called. I do not know what to say. How could I tell her that her brother, whom she adores and loves so much, told me to stay away?"

"Silver," Nick began. "No more. You have been quiet and withdrawn since you came back, and it's time you admitted to yourself that you're in love. You are deeply, madly, head over heels in love with Willow Rainey Dawson. The sooner you admit it, the happier the staff will be, including myself, and most importantly, so will you. I just want to know why are you still here?"

Silver laughed and smiled. Silver had known as soon as he had left Willow that morning and returned to Landon's home that he was in love with her. He did not just love Willow, but it was the heart hurting, heading spinning in love with her. What made it even worse was the fact that when Silver returned, Landon confirmed it as well. First, he had apologized to Silver and told him he had known for quite some time his little sister had been smitten with Silver.

Landon's exact words were, "I knew she had already fallen in love with you by just seeing the way she looked at you that morning, when you left."

Silver had told his best friend he appreciated the apology. He had promised he would never intentionally make Willow another notch on his belt, but out of respect for Willow, their parents, and their friendship, he would not pursue a relationship. Landon had fallen into a fit of laughter and had told Silver before leaving, "It's too late. She's captured your heart with her kind, caring, compassionate personality. It's okay to admit you've fallen in love with her. I think the entire family knew and had hoped this would happen. We all just needed to allow the good Lord to step in with His timing."

And now, Silver was still thinking about Willow Rainey Dawson. Wondering if she felt the same way as he did. Nick punched Silver in the arm.

"I've seen that look. That was my look with Winter. Good lord, man, just get in your truck and leave. You will never know unless you see her face to face. If, when she sees you, she looks deep in your eyes and you cannot turn away, then it's real. There will be no words that need to be spoken. If your heart flutters and feels like it will never stop, then it's real.

Dr. Silver Bleu, you are smitten and deeply in love with Willow. I'm not going to let you off the hook until I see you leaving the hospital and headed back to Blessings."

Silver smiled. He knew exactly what Nick was talking about. And he knew what his next step was. Before he could overthink, Silver looked at Nick and said, "I'll send you an invitation."

Nick chuckled. "You better. I'm counting on a road trip to the mountains."

CHAPTER 31

Silver drove home, jumped out of his truck, briskly walked through his front door, and began packing as much as what he thought he needed to make the trip to Blessings and to surprise Willow with his feelings. Lord, this was going to be one for the books. Silver felt nervous, a foreign emotion. He was always in control of any and all decisions, but this one decision had him stumbling around his bedroom. He hurriedly finished his packing and made the flight reservations online. Then, out the door he went. He took one look back and smiled. His future was waiting in Blessings.

Silver had called Landon to confirm that Willow had returned to their parents' home. He landed in Blessings around one o'clock their time. The desire to see Willow had given Silver a rush of adrenaline. He practically ran to the rental car lot. As he pulled out of the lot, Silver pulled out his phone and found the address to Willow's parents' house and began the journey.

He let himself enjoy the drive to Willow's parent's home. He rolled the windows down and placed his left arm on the outside to feel the warmth of the rays glistening down.

As he turned into their rocky driveway, Silver's heart began to beat faster than normal. He drove up and saw Willow's parents outside walking hand in hand. Landon had told Silver that in a few short months, their parents would be celebrating their 40th wedding anniversary. Landon and Willow had planned a huge surprise celebration with family and friends. Silver smiled. He wanted what Willow's parents had – plain and simple love. He wanted it with Willow.

Willow's parents saw the SUV pull into the driveway. They did not recognize the vehicle as belonging to any of their friends or family at first, but as they drew closer, Willow's dad squeezed Willow's mom's hand and whispered, "I knew he would come back."

She laughed and said, "Now did you? I was getting a bit concerned. It took him long enough. We aren't getting any younger."

Silver watched as they approached the SUV. They were smiling and laughing with each other. He opened the door and extended his hand to Willow's dad.

Before Silver could say anything, Willow's dad said, "What took you so long? I don't know how much longer her mother and I could take her moping around here like a lovesick puppy." Silver could not help but smile from ear to ear. She had missed him.

Willow's mom hooked hers with Silver's and said, "Let's go inside and get a bite to eat. I was just about to, and now you can join us." How could Silver turn Willow's mom down?

They all sat down to eat, and they immediately launched into their questions about how he was doing, how was the hospital, what new remarkable medical innovations were up and coming began. He knew that Willow's mom and dad were making small talk with Silver and he truly relished the fact that they cared enough to do so.

No one heard the noise of a car travelling down the rock road. No one heard the door slam to a vehicle. No one heard her until she called, "

Mom, Dad, I'm home!"

Both Willow's parents looked at Silver expectantly. Silver knew there was no way of escape now. He would have to face the music. Silver chuckled. He was trapped inside the home of the parents of the woman he was in love with. This could not get any more comical than at this moment.

To Silver's chagrin, it did get more comical. As soon as the door opened, they all stood up in anticipation because they did not know how Willow would react to Silver's arrival.

Willow walked in and immediately froze in shock. Before anyone could say anything, she burst out, "Are you serious? He's here? What's he doing here? How long has he been here? What have you been talking about?"

Before anyone could answer the questions that were being fired one after another, Willow's dad grabbed Willow's mother's hand and said, "I think we need to take a stroll outside and …"

"And what?" Willow asked. "Leave me here with him?" She pointed her finger in Silver's direction. Her parents looked at each other and then at Willow.

"Yep, that's exactly what we are going to do. We are going to take a little walk outside on our farm," her dad replied. Willow's dad turned his head and winked at Silver. "Just so you know, you're in for it now. But I know you can fix this."

Silver could not believe they were going to leave him alone with Willow who visibly was literally madder than a wet hen. Silver nodded and mouthed a thank you to them. Willow's parents then walked out the door. It was only Silver and Willow. She was standing in front of him with both hands on her hips. This was not going to go well, Silver thought to himself.

CHAPTER 32

"Good afternoon, Willow. How has your day been?" Silver knew that sometimes being polite could break the ice. He was willing to try anything to cool the look Willow was giving him.

"Oh, no. You're not getting out of this so easy. You're not leaving here until I get answers from you. You're trapped. You're caught. You're here. I would suggest you have seat at the kitchen table. Silver knew he had some explaining to do. How was he going to tell Willow he was in love with her? He drank in the sight of her. He loved how when she got mad, she placed her hands on her hips, like a cheerleader. He loved how when she was unsure of herself, she bit her bottom lip. He loved how when she did not know what to say, she would pop her knuckles. He loved every inch of her.

Willow walked towards him, pointing her finger at his chest. "You left me. You left me without an explanation. You left me no time to even ask, why? I just want to know why."

Before he answered, Silver took one step, pulled Willow close to him, and kissed her. He kissed her as if he would never see her again. She gasped, and Silver took the opportunity to slide his tongue inside her mouth to taste what he had been missing for several months. Silver felt her body respond. Their kiss deepened. Willow felt like her body had betrayed her. She had wanted to be strong and let Silver know she was not happy with him. Instead, the kiss had melted her body into his arms and had allowed him access to the sweetness of her tongue. She never knew the lips or tongue could bring this kind of satisfaction. She did not want the kiss to stop. But she needed to stop. She needed answers, and Silver was not getting off this easily.

"Silver, stop. I need to know. Please, answer my question," Willow pleaded.

"I know you need answers. What I'm about to tell you is the truth. When your brother found out what had happened between you and I, he asked me not to hurt you. I hope you know I never meant to leave without talking to you or explaining how I was feeling. He told me he did not want me to make you another "notch in my belt". I thought I was making a decision that was best for everyone. I left and went back to Pioneer Children's Hospital. It finally took a friend of mine to help me realize all my moping was because of you."

"'All your moping was because of me'," Willow repeated. She began to smile. "Silver tell me why you were moping? Remember, truth," Willow told him.

"Truth is, I thought of you constantly. I wondered what you were doing. I wondered if you had forgotten about that night. I wondered if you had forgotten about me. Everyone at the hospital saw what I did not want to admit."

Willow stopped Silver by placing her fingers on his lips. "What did you not want to admit, Silver? Tell me."

Silver took Willow's two small fingers and kissed each one and pulled her closer to him. "Willow Rainey Dawson, I love you. Three words that I thought I would never say. An emotion that was unknown to me until I met you. Pioneer Children's Hospital cannot wait to meet the woman who has stolen my heart. And I cannot wait to introduce them to you."

Willow stepped back. "You're in love with me? I sure wished you would have let me in on this secret you have kept."

"I am. I'm telling you right here and right now – I am in love with you." He touched the side of her face.

He started to ask why she had not said it back, but Willow laughed and said, "Took you long enough. Silver Bleu, these last few months have been pure torture. I did not want to interfere in your professional or personal life, and just like you, I threw myself into my job. There was not a second that I did not think about you and if I should call you. I am in love with you, Dr. Bleu. So now what do you think you're gonna do?"

Standing there waiting for Willow's reply, it felt as if time was standing still. He grabbed Willow's hand and replied, "I'm going to kiss you into tomorrow, and then kiss you all over again. I'll never stop kissing you, Willow. This moment is my forever. You are my forever."

Willow blushed and whispered into Silver's ear, "You are my today and tomorrow. I cannot wait to see where the journey leads us. I am yours, Silver."

Outside, Willow's parents had overheard their entire conversation. Willow's dad and mom hugged each other tightly. Thank goodness Willow and Silver had come to the realization that love exists and does conquer all. Willow's parents were ready to come inside and congratulate the couple because it had turned into a smouldering day.

It had risen two degrees hotter.

DE DE COX

"Born and raised in Rooster Run, Kentucky, Deanna (de de) Cox, grew up reading romance novels. She and her sister, Casonya, would discuss the books and ponder what they would write, if the opportunity ever arose. At the age of 30, de de began to write her first romance book. But as in life, circumstances change and life moves you in a different direction. The direction led de de into the charitable industry, due to the upbringing of her Grandma Bea. She is actively involved in Make a Wish Foundation, Blessings in a Backpack, Spalding University, Toys for Tots, The Molly Johnson Foundation, Indiana Bulldog Rescue Foundation and volunteers with numerous other charities. She is a prelim director in the festival and America pageant system. She is also the Executive Co-Director of the Miss Kentucky Junior High, High School and Collegiate America state pageant. At the mature age of 35, her only child was born, Isaiah Bo. His name is taken from Isaiah 40:31. Bo is the actual cover model for the books *Two Degrees One Heart, the Perfect Chrystmas and now, Two Degrees Hotter.* When de de began writing the book, she had no idea she would have a son, and never imagined Bo would be on the cover - a book she had written before he was even born. de de feels that everything is in God's timing. Her second son, Matthew Tracy, came into her life to complete her family. She has been married to Scott Cox, her best friend from high school, for over 30 years. We are a society that impatiently waits for patience. de de continues her passion of writing romance books, for where would the world be without love? Never forget Acts 20:35."

de de Cox

TWO DEGREES
ONE HEART

It was going to be one of those Monday mornings. As Logan was jogging into the hospital entrance, he could see several others were in his dilemma. Running a bit behind. It was Logan's first day of his new travel assignment. He did not want to be late. Logan knew the first impression was the lasting impression.

Winter knew she could not turn away. This was the man she was in love with. This was the man she wanted to spend the rest of her life with.

CPSIA information can be obtained
at www.ICGtesting.com
Printed in the USA
FSHW020609100320
67969FS